I0640245

THE FISHER KING'S APPRENTICE

A R HORVATH

From the Annals of Myrtle
and the Blood-King

2.

Published By

ATHANATOS
PUBLISHING GROUP

FISHER KING'S APPRENTICE

A R HORVATH

From the Annals of Myrtle
and the Blood-King

2.

ATHANATOS
PUBLISHING GROUP

The Fisher King's Apprentice
By AR Horvath

ISBN: 978-1-64594-226-9

Also available in hard cover at ISBN: 978-1-64594-225-2

And as an e-book at ISBN: 978-1-64594-227-6

Copyright 2024 by AR Horvath. All Rights Reserved.

To learn more about the *Annals of Myrtle and the Blood-King* visit: www.thebloodking.com.

How *You* Can Help The Author

The reader may not realize it, but the way books are made, bought, and sold, has changed quite a bit. In the old days, books were bought in bookstores. Today, they are bought over the Internet. In an earlier time, people heard about books in newspapers and magazines. That still happens, of course, but now people hear about books in many other ways, such as through social media. In some ways, that is good for authors. They do not have to pay a lot of money to get heard. There are challenges though: *everyone* is trying to get heard! With all that 'noise,' it can be hard for the authors you enjoy to get noticed.

That's where you come in.

If you enjoy what you are about to read, and want to read more by the author, you can help. How? Tell *everyone* you know about the book. That is a great start.

To learn more about how you can spread the word about this book, be sure to check out the section at the end where more ideas are given.

I hope you enjoy *The Fisher King's Apprentice*, the second in the *Annals of Myrtle and the Blood-King*. After this (or before, if you like!) enjoy the first in the *Annals, The Warden-Watch*.

Sincerely,
AR Horvath

The Turks, however, engaged them in battle and by shooting killed many of our men. Other squadrons, moreover, were drawn out from the river to the mountain, which was about two miles distant. The squadrons began to go forth from both sides and to surround our men on all sides, hurling, shooting, and wounding them. There came out from the mountains, also, countless armies with white horses, whose standards were all white. And so, when our leaders saw this army, they were entirely ignorant as to what it was, and who they were, until they recognized the aid of Christ, whose leaders were St. George, Mercurius, and Demetrius. This is to be believed, for many of our men saw it.

From the *Gesta Francorum*, c. 1100 AD. As found in *The First Crusade: The Accounts of Eyewitnesses and Participants* by August C. Krey, 1921.

There was a certain pilgrim of our army, whose name was Peter [Bartholomew], to whom before we entered the city St. Andrew, the apostle, appeared and said: "What art thou doing, good man?" Peter answered, "Who art thou?" The apostle said to him: "I am St. Andrew, the apostle. Know, my son, that when thou shalt enter the town, go to the church of St. Peter. There thou wilt find the Lance of our Saviour, Jesus Christ, with which He was wounded as He hung on the arm of the cross." Having said all this, the apostle straightway withdrew.

But Peter, afraid to reveal the advice of the apostle, was unwilling to make it known to the pilgrims. However, he thought that he had seen a vision, and said: "Lord, who would believe this?" But at that hour St. Andrew took him and carried him to the place where the Lance was hidden in the ground. When we were a second time situated in such (straits) as we have stated above, St. Andrew came again, saying to him: "Wherefore hast thou not yet taken the Lance from the earth as I commanded thee? Know, verily, that whoever shall bear this lance in battle shall never be overcome by an enemy." Peter, indeed, straightway made known to our men the mystery of the apostle.

The people, however, did not believe (it), but refused, saying: "How can we believe this?" For they were utterly terrified and thought that they were to die forthwith. Thereupon, this man came forth and swore that it was all most true, since St. Andrew had twice appeared to him in a vision and had said to him: "Rise, go and tell the people of God not to fear, but to trust firmly with whole heart in the one true God and they will be everywhere victorious. Within five days the Lord will send them such a token that they will remain happy and joyful, and if they wish to fight, let them go out immediately to battle, all together, and all their enemies will be conquered, and no one will stand against them."

Thereupon, when they heard that their enemies were to be overcome by them, they began straightway to revive and to encourage one another, saying: "Bestir yourselves, and be everywhere brave and alert, since the Lord will come to our aid in the next battle and will be the greatest refuge to His people whom He beholds lingering in sorrow."

Accordingly, upon hearing the statements of that man who reported to us the revelation of Christ through the words of the apostle, we went in haste immediately to the place in the church of St. Peter which he had pointed out. Thirteen men dug there from morning until vespers. And so that man found the Lance, just as he had indicated. They received it with great gladness and fear, and a joy beyond measure arose in the whole city.

From the *Gesta Francorum*, c. 1100 AD. As found in *The First Crusade: The Accounts of Eyewitnesses and Participants* by August C. Krey, 1921.

CHAPTER 1

Books, books, and more books. Books on books, books in books, books about books. Books.

Books had been at the center of my life for more than a year. As one of the few people on the earth to have stumbled upon the truth about Big Foot—by actually stumbling *upon* Big Foot—I did not expect as my reward to have my nose inside a book indefinitely.

I had been led to believe that I was going to be embarking on a great adventure. The reality, thus far, was mundane, to say the least.

It all began when I was twelve. I had been minding my own business when I spotted a mysterious shadow. After sneaking up on it, I pounced, only to lay hands on a giant, hairy creature. I soon discovered that these creatures were called 'Wardens,' and their task was to open and close the 'gates' in and out of our own realm as angels, fallen and otherwise, did battle.

One thing led to another, and I ended up meeting the world's oldest woman, and was there when she was restored to her youth by eating the fruit of the Tree of Life. Not long after that, I found myself in her service, seeking to thwart the plots of the world's oldest man, who, not coincidentally, was the husband of the aforementioned woman. Her name was Myrtle, and his name was Draco.

Heaping adventure upon adventure, I accompanied Myrtle through the Warden's 'Time' Tunnels into a past present... and not just any past present... but one that served as a pivot for all of history. I was in Jerusalem on the day that Jesus was crucified. My job? To prevent Draco from collecting any of Jesus' blood, which he would have used for his own devilish purposes. I bungled the job, but how badly was yet to be determined. At any rate, the blood that I kept out of Draco's hands ended up in a clay jar, and from there... lost. But at least not in *his* hands!

My new quest centered upon discovering the location of the 'holy grail' in this *present* present. I expected this to mean traveling across the world wearing a fedora hat and carrying a whip, but instead I was sent to a sprawling estate in South Carolina, and plopped into a large house with a large library, surrounded by trees, brooks, and ponds. And armed guards. As one of only three people on the planet that knew the true nature of the 'holy grail,' it was imperative that I was kept safe.

In that time, I never saw Myrtle once. I shouldn't complain. I remembered well my last exchange with her before I was swooped away:

"So, what next?" I inquired.
"Draco—for that is what I call him now—will do what he can to find us, so we need not

pursue him. We shall begin by trying to locate the Two Trees. If we can destroy them, we will strike a singular blow to his ambitions," Myrtle answered.

"And where should we look first?" I pressed.

"In the local library," Myrtle said matter-of-factly.

"That doesn't sound exciting," I remarked in disbelief.

"Like you said, Casey. You're only twelve-years old. Do you think I'd allow you to put yourself on the front lines, somewhere? I will have violated your parents' trust if I did something like that. No, young man. You have much to learn first, and it will take you the better part of the decade. At that point perhaps you'll get your fill of excitement. But never you worry: just by being associated with me you are in danger. You will just have to satisfy yourself with the knowledge that opening up a book on my behalf may still get you killed. That's excitement enough, for now," Myrtle said, a slight smile playing on her face.

"So, the library," I sighed. "And where does one begin looking for such trees in a library?"

"Oh heavens, Casey! First you have to know all sorts of *other* things before you can do something like that! You need to pick up some foreign languages, master some archeology, geology, geography, anthropology, physics, chemistry, literature, and so on and so forth!"

Myrtle clapped her hand on my shoulder.

"Why? For what?" I protested.

"We have access to the best libraries in the world. You're as likely to find your clue written in ancient hieroglyphs as you are to find it in a Polish newspaper from the 1800s as you are to find it in English lore. Young sir, you will practically be an expert in *everything* by the time that we're done with you!" Myrtle comforted me.

"Well, for you, Myrtle, I'd practically do anything. If for now all you ask is that I study hard, I will do it gladly," I surrendered.

"That's the spirit!" Myrtle exclaimed.

"You're right," inserted her bodyguard and chauffer, Mr. Chaffee. "This one is different."

∞ ∞ ∞

The enthusiasm behind my vow to gladly study cooled fairly rapidly after a few months of putting my money where my mouth was. Indeed, whenever I recall that she had said I would have to be studying for nearly ten years before actually doing anything, I get grumpy. Being largely alone, there was no one to be snippy to, but I sure wished there had been.

But if you had ever seen Myrtle face to face, you would understand how one would be willing to make any vow or launch upon any crusade. One twinkle of her eye, one gesture of a finger—your heart sank in despair if you saw her mouth exhibiting anything but mirth. Yet, if you thought about it, it was not only her body that was rejuvenated by the Tree of Life but also her mind. I then should not have been surprised when she knew full well what my limits were and, just when I had reached them, altered the arrangements.

After about four months of being virtually alone with little direction, Mr. Chaffee, the gruff but loyal chauffer, bodyguard, and confidant to Myrtle, strode through the door and hailed me from the foyer.

"Caaaa-sey!" he hollered.

I bounded down the ornate steps, spewing books and notepads as I went. I embraced the man, who had become as an uncle to me. You would think that a rough person like Mr. Chaffee would have recoiled at the affection, but he did not, picking me up and giving me a bear hug in return. After a moment, he set me down, and you could not guess from his face that he'd ever experienced anything as sentimental as the hug he had just administered.

Mr. Chaffee let me lead him to the kitchen via my offer to give him a drink and a snack, but he was not the sort to deal in pleasantries. He got right to the point.

"You will be returning to your family for a time, Casey," he said.

"What? I thought I was going to be meeting others like me, but instead I've been living in this giant house, alone, reading," I replied.

"You will be meeting others like you, but the time

must be right. They are more advanced in their training than you, but they lack something that you still need, and to be perfectly blunt, it is the presence of your parents on a regular basis. We let you stew here at the estate for a while as a test, and you did fine, and the plan continues to look promising. Part of that plan, however, is that you continue your education, but from your home, with your family," he explained.

Now, I missed my family terribly, and didn't mind if anyone knew it. That said, I had been under the distinct impression I would be hanging out with cool people and then seeing the world. I assumed these things would be happening at the same time. So, I was a bit put off to discover that I was now simply going home.

"I don't understand," I whined. "I know I'm ready to get out there and take on the world!"

Mr. Chaffee was not one to beat around the bush, "You are only fourteen, Casey. In the real world, teenagers don't have the answers to questions that adults themselves haven't been able to find. If anything, most adults wish that they had been better prepared for the complexities that real life presents to them. It is just that preparation that you will be receiving. Did you not happily pledge to do Myrtle's bidding, even if her bidding was to be bored?"

It bothered me to admit that he was right, so all I did was mumble under my breath.

Mr. Chaffee smiled, "Well said."

"So, what, then?" I asked.

"I will take you home. You will be given a reading list this time, but you must also read the books that your father sets before you. He has been around the block a few times. You have only been out the door and to the street and back. Never fear, though. After another few months, I will fetch you again. And there is something else."

"Yes?"

"You need to start doing some push-ups, young man. Those arms are starting to look a little like tooth-picks!"

I laughed and punched him in the shoulder, and that giant of a man pretended to cry.

CHAPTER 2.

Mr. Chaffee had not been kidding about the push-ups.

Once returned to my family, I was given a long list of books to read as well as a list of physical exercises to do. I didn't mind the books, but chafed a bit at the exercises. I would only do them if someone hounded me to do them, and they often forgot to do this.

It was nice to be back on the homestead. My siblings knew that I had a special arrangement set up, and let me be to do my readings, but then when I had had about as much I could stand, I would go out and play with them. In the old days, I probably wouldn't have had much time for my siblings. The time away, however, had reminded me anew that I kinda liked them.

First was Sydney, now nine, and soon to be ten. Then Jessica, who was seven or eight, I could never remember. My twin brothers, Maxwell and Samuel, had just turned eighteen. We played a little football on the lawn here and there, but they were getting ready to go off to college and were a little pre-occupied. In fact, my oldest brother, Tom, was already at college.

Just as it seemed everything was falling into a routine, the few months were up, and Mr. Chaffee came to fetch me again. I was returned to the estate. As before, I was left alone, although this time I had a reading list. I also had a stern warning from Mr. Chaffee to do my exercises. As I wandered the estate house I had the distinct impression that someone else had been making use of it while I was gone. Books were not where I had left them and I would find items left in weird places, much like when I had been there, I would leave my empty glass of milk on a window sill and forget about it.

Soon enough, I was alone with the books, *again*. Once again, just as it seemed I had reached the limits of loneliness, I heard calling from the foyer, "Casey, dear child, where are you?"

It was Myrtle's crystal voice breaking through the double-wooden doors of the estate house even before they were opened. I sprung up from where I was sitting, surrounded on all sides by towers of stacked books. Apart from the chef and one of the guards, I had not spoken to anyone for a week, and by that time had not seen Myrtle for a year. The sound that reached my ears was not that of a word spoken, but rather a song sung. The singing solo mysteriously harmonized with itself. My loneliness melted away as if I had never been alone in my life.

I ran to greet her, but she was upon me before I had made it five steps. She hugged me tight and probably would have gone on doing so except other voices came upon the heels of hers, and soon I recognized who they belonged to—my family!

Jessica and Sydney both hugged, me, but

sauntering along nonchalantly, as if bored already, were Max and Sam. Mom and Dad followed close behind, prodding the twins along. Sam patted me on the back, as if fulfilling his minimum obligations, while Max punched me in the shoulder and grinned. The two smelled food and disappeared in search of it, leaving my folks to have their turn hugging me.

"Shall we go to the library?" Myrtle suggested.

I led the way.

In my months and months of study, one thing I had learned from history is that siblings didn't much appreciate each other until after they had matured a bit more. Not that I was much better; but then, I had been in isolation for so long, I would have welcomed almost anyone's company—even that of my older brothers! They found us in the library, each with a plate of cookies, chips and sweet rolls, the sight of which prompted my sisters to disappear in search of their own.

"I missed you all so much," I said.

"We missed you, too, Casey," Mom said, dabbing away at her eyes.

"Mom…" I said, almost embarrassed. "You just saw me a few months ago."

"I know, I know," she said, dabbing away.

"What brings you here just now? No one told me you were coming!" I asked them.

"Myrtle told us you were going on a trip, and said it would be good to see you off, since it could be a long while before we see you again," Dad explained.

I laughed and looked at Myrtle, who was grinning at me, "She hasn't said anything to *me* about it!"

"You were busy," she said.

I laughed again, "I'm not so sure about that."

Honestly, I would have been irritated, even angry, had it been anyone else, but it was impossible to be even slightly annoyed around Myrtle. I let it go.

"We're going to be staying for a few days," Dad continued. "I hope you don't mind."

"Not at all," I said. "Would you like a tour?"

Sam and Max's expression changed and Sydney squealed with delight.

"Absolutely," Mom said. "I'd love to see how you've been spending your time. We even missed your fourteenth birthday!"

"No worries!" I exclaimed. "Let me show you around!"

Myrtle hung back behind the group as I led the way around the massive house. The library in the house was large and ornate, but they had already seen that, of course, so I took them to the large ballroom next. They 'ooohed' and 'ahhed' at the chandeliers. Then I showed them the dining room and the kitchen my siblings had already discovered. I was a little embarrassed about the mess that I had made everywhere but perplexed as to how the island had suddenly become stocked with all sorts of snacks and goodies. Mounds of shirts and socks were strewn about, naturally, but I realized that in the monotony I had also littered the whole place with books as I moved from place to place reading them, changing up the scenery to keep me alert. Then I took them to see my bedroom.

"Your bedroom is bigger than our whole house," Sydney said in amazement. I hadn't really thought about it in a long time. I was a little ashamed that I had enjoyed such luxury without even appreciating it, but my dad, apparently seeing me shifting uncomfortably, put me at ease.

"Don't worry, son. As you know, thanks to Myrtle's intercessions, our financial circumstances have changed greatly for the better. We are all quite comfortable."

"Check this out!" I said, moving aside a bookcase. Behind it, a secret passageway was revealed.

"Where does it go?" Sam said, pushing me aside. Max was by me before I could reply.

"Everywhere!" I said. "Go check it out!"

Soon, the whole family was in the passageway. It split off into numerous directions and each person took a different passage as they explored. I could hear excited shouts from all corners of the house as they discovered new entries and exits. Briefly, I was alone with Myrtle as we tried to keep up with the family.

"I'm going on a trip?" I asked, glancing at her as we walked.

"Yep, it's time. Besides, you needed a break from your studies," she said.

"I'll say," I chuckled.

"Your family will stay for two days. On the third, Mr. Chafee will drop by and he'll explain everything after that."

"I suppose you won't tell me anything else until then?" I cocked my head at her.

"For the safety of your family, I think no," she said. My interest was really piqued now, but I knew better than to try to extract anything else from her. We caught up to my Mom and Dad at last, and, forgetting my own curiosity, set my mind to enjoying the company of my family for the next couple of days.

On the evening before the morning my family was to leave, I left the den where I was playing a board game with my siblings in search of a snack. As I navigated the hallway, I heard voices in a distant room. Myrtle, Mr. Chaffee, and my parents were talking. I was about to make my presence known and then I heard my name dropped, and it was in a serious tone. I stopped a little way from the room they were in and tried to gauge from the conversation if they had heard I was nearby. It seemed that they had not.

"For this reason, we have to be cautious going forward," Myrtle was saying. "Casey is a special young man, but the more he comes to realize that—

and certainly the more we tell him that—the easier the slide into arrogance that all teenagers are vulnerable of falling into."

I could see my father nodding in my mind's eye as he replied, "With three boys older than Casey, we've already seen a fair bit of the 'we already know everything' schtick."

"It will be much worse for Casey, though," she said. "I have seen cases where a gifted young man or woman, even having seen great wonders, forgets them all. They despise their parents, and discount their own experiences. The life we live is in many important ways a life of obedience to God, and when you are as smart as they are… or think they are… they see no reason anymore to obey anyone, not even their own Maker. All the more once they discover some of the pleasures of life which their Maker has arranged for them to enjoy… in moderation or in proper context."

There was a heavy moment of silence. I thought perhaps the lack of reply from my parents was due to confusion. Although I knew Myrtle to be more than two thousand years old, as far as my parents knew, Myrtle was only a few years older than my oldest brother, Tom, who was still in college. My parents did not know about the Tree of Life or Time Tunnels.

At last, I heard my father say, "What, then, do you propose?"

"Well, there is probably nothing more humbling than to be around people who are bigger and better than you are. At the earliest chance, we will mix Casey in with some of those. The problem is that Casey is still only fourteen. He isn't quite old enough and mature enough to have his lot thrown in with them. Special he is—but so are they."

"And so?" my mother urged Myrtle on.

"We will continue the cycle. A few months here in study followed by a few months at home, then a few months of study, and then we take him out in the 'field,' as it were. We let him interact with some of his future peers, and then we do it all over again."

"I am encouraged by your wisdom," my dad said. "It eases my mind knowing he will not be thrown into something before he is ready."

"No one is ever ready," Mr. Chaffee replied, but Myrtle cut him off before he could say anything else.

"—But we will try to equip him the best we can nonetheless," she said.

Sensing the conversation was coming to an end, I tip-toed away, certain, for some reason, that my mother was once again dabbing her eyes. It was a lot for me to think about. When I returned to my siblings to finish our board game, I was lost in my thoughts, and promptly defeated. I didn't mind. I was ready to lay in bed and ponder matters as I fell asleep.

CHAPTER 3.

Was it the smell of fish? The scent of the sea? Perhaps it was the sound of a boat thudding against a dock that woke me. Whatever it was, despite being deep asleep, something had awakened me abruptly. It was still dark outside, so that the only light in my bedroom was coming from a nightlight on the far side of the room.

I suppose everyone knows how it is when they are awakened in the middle of the night. The fleeting remnants of a vivid dream rush away as the real world floods in, but one is still in such a stupor that you can't hardly tell the difference between the dream you were having and the room you are in. It was like that for me at that moment. My eyes slowly opened. As they did, I beheld in silhouette a large, shifting shape, standing over me, which my mind struggled to interpret.

Just as it was dawning on me that the shape was a man standing over me with some kind of weapon above his head, I heard him shout, "Die, thief!" The weapon, whatever it was, came swinging down and plunged into the pillow, right where my head had been.

"Jesus Christ!" I screamed. It was not profanity. As in the millions of other cases where someone had terror suddenly come upon them simultaneous to the recognition that no mortal salvation was available to them, I called upon the only one I knew who could save me at that moment. I did not call upon Muhammed or Joseph Smith or Charles Darwin— nobody on the planet in such circumstances ever did. I was not taking the name of the Lord in vain. I really meant it, just as everyone else did… in such moments.

I had rolled away from the blow and in the dark kept rolling before I could get to my feet. I felt the wind of another swing coming towards me and ducked instinctively as I heard the object strike the wall. As the cobwebs in my mind fled for their own lives, I concluded that the man was wielding an axe. I shouted again, "Help! HELP!"

My bedroom door opened, allowing light from the hallway to enter the room. I was able to see my assailant with more detail. He was large—larger than Mr. Chaffee, for sure. He had long hair that seemed unkempt as it fell below the shoulders. He was wearing a long, flowing garment, cinched around his waist with a rope. And he was definitely swinging an axe.

I rushed to the door, discovering that the one who had opened it was my sister, Sydney.

"Are you ok, Casey?" she asked softly.

I grabbed hold of her arm, clad in a loose pajama top, and shouted, "Run!"

My attacker was close on our heels as I pulled Sydney along. There definitely was a smell about the man and it definitely was something similar to what I had smelled on a trip with my family once to a wharf. The smell caught me before the man did; he had to be nearly on top of me. I took a sharp turn into an empty doorway, still hauling my sister with me. The man, surprised at the sudden change of direction, continued past the doorway before catching himself.

It was all the time I needed, though. The old grandfather clock that served as the doorway to one of the estate's secret tunnels had just closed, with me and my sis in the tunnel, as he entered the room.

"THIEF!" he shouted. "Where are you, HEATHEN?"

I put my hand over Sydney's mouth to keep her from screaming and tried to silence my own heart which was hammering inside my body so loudly I could barely hear my own breathing. I knew it was only a matter of time before the intruder figured things out, so I forced myself to think.

"We've got to keep moving," I whispered to Sydney. It was pitch black in the tunnel, leaving me to thread my way through as carefully as I could to avoid making too much noise. There were lights in the tunnel, but in my haste, I had failed to throw the switch. Inevitably, we knocked up against a wall, and very quickly after that I heard the grandfather clock opening again. The attacker shouted "Aha!" and he, unlike me, did take the time to search for the light switch. The lights came on in the tunnel, hurting my eyes badly and leaving me and Sydney trapped and at his mercy.

For the first time, I got a full, albeit brief, look at my attacker. He was a head taller than my own father. The face looked aged, adorned with an unkempt dirty grey beard down past his neck. The long hair on his head was the same color, and was matted into knots here and there. His plain, grey cloak was indeed tightened by a thick rope. His pants were loose-fitting and tucked into boots that ended just before the knee-caps. I took all this in at a glance, because my attention was drawn to the most compelling feature—the axe he was carrying in his hand. I recognized it as the axe in the 'break in case of emergency' box mounted inside the walk-in freezer in the kitchen.

"Aha!" the man yelled again, leaping for us. I wasn't going to let him be the only one doing any leaping today, so I increased my grip on Sydney's arm and lurched down the secret passageway. We were only ten feet away from our demise, and the distance was shrinking rapidly.

I turned a corner in the tunnel, and as I did, I saw a rift in space that I had seen a few times before in my life. Out of that rift, the beautiful hairy face of my old friend Marmor appeared. The smell of freshly baked bread slammed into the smell of a fish market. In my mind, the scents did battle, buying me critical time.

"Quickly, Casey!" he ordered, reaching out and yanking me into the rift, which sealed tightly behind me. I was once again surrounded in the darkest of darks. I knew it was one of the Time Tunnels of the Mammalites, who I knew better as the Warden-Watchers or Gate Wardens, or simply, the Wardens. I also knew that if I had the sight to see it, these tunnels would be lit with light brighter than any light visible on earth save the sun itself. But that sight was available by special dispensation of their king. Would I once again be favored to receive it?

CHAPTER 4.

"And that," I said, "is how I came to be in the Great Cavern Council of the Wardens."

I was explaining myself to an assembly of large, hairy creatures, that I knew were the source for the legend of 'Big Foot.' I was standing in the middle of a circle of their elders. Marmor, who had pulled me into their realm, was sitting in a circle, too, but his circle was a great distance from mine. He had his head buried in his hands and was rocking back and forth in apparent shame.

"You put us in an impossible situation, Daughter of Eve," a voice declared, emanating from the far end of the Grand Cavern.

"Say what?" I said incredulously. "Daughter of Eve? I'm a Son of Adam, don't you remember?"

Now another voice spoke, "For thousands of years the Wardens have been hidden from the sight of your race, and only because of this do we Wardens continue to survive. If you were to depart from us, untold harm could come to us."

"Yet, she cannot stay!" declared another.

"An impossible situation," repeated the first voice.

"What is going on?" I said, probably a little too boldly. It was all very perplexing, given the fact that I already had heard this speech before.

"She must be put to death," said the one that had said my sister couldn't stay.

"She has done nothing to warrant that sentence," the first voice said.

"And what about *him?*" said the one who wanted… someone… not me, apparently… dead. If it wasn't me the speaker had in mind, I knew he must be referring to Marmor.

"He also has done nothing to warrant death," a voice said.

"An impossible situation!" voices from the black began calling out, until at last their voices fell into sync, turning into a low, gravely hum, "Uh-Hummah-Hum-Hum-Hummah." I recalled well that deep rhythm and how it seemed to resonate inside my very bones.

A small cone of light illuminated my circle, and now the one I knew to be the king of the Wardens stepped into it. He put his hand over my eyes. As he pulled his hand away, I could see the Warden-Realm in all its brilliance, just as I had before.

"Are they going to kill me?" a girl's voice whispered plaintively. I was now able to see that Sydney was with me. The chain of events that must have unfolded appeared in my mind's eye: Marmor grabbed me, but so did Sydney. I was pulled through the gate, but so, too, was Sydney. *I* was part of the plan, but Sydney was unexpected. Marmor had done it again! He had brought unbidden another human to the Warden's Keep!

There was mirth and sadness combined in the

eyes of the King as he regarded me. As he looked upon me, he shook his head. I had seen this expression before, on my father's face. (Many times, actually.) It was the look on my father's face when I had done something not just monumentally stupid, but when I had done it *again*, after having known better.

The King turned his gaze upon Marmor. "What am I going to do with you?" he said, shaking his head. Then he turned his attention to Sydney, who was huddled on her knees next to my legs. "And what am I going to do with *you*?" he asked her.

I saw Marmor turn his head my way. I locked eyes with him, and I could tell that they told a tale that I myself could tell; they said, "I can't believe I did it again!"

Having gone through this before, I knew what the problem was. The secret of the Wardens was closely kept, as the Wardens provided a valuable service to the world. It was their job to hold open, and close when needed, the gates through which angelic messengers and warriors—good and bad—entered and exited. Yet, the Mammalites were also hunted by Man. There had never been a wondrous creature that humans had not killed for the mere pleasure of killing. If humanity learned about the Wardens, it would stop at nothing in its quest to discover their lair, and empty it, by whatever means necessary.

The Wardens serve humans, but their tunnels

were not made for humans. My first arrival to their realm had confronted them with a serious problem. If they sent me back into my world, would I not eventually spill the beans, and put not just them at risk, but the entire world?

I knelt before the King and bowed my head low… even though I knew that the Wardens hated when I did this. "My king, please spare my sister. We were both running for our very lives, and Marmor, who was sent by Jesus himself to rescue me, could not have known what would happen, and if he had known, would have done it anyway, and would have been right to do it."

The King grabbed me by the shoulders and forced me to stand. "She shall redeem herself as you are redeeming yourself, by working to unravel at least some of the harm that you both shall inflict in the future. To save ourselves, we might want to bring judgement upon you, but this, we know, would bring even greater judgement upon ourselves. We must therefore endure the troubles that will befall us, by no fault of our own."

"But—" interjected a voice. It was the one that had called for our deaths to begin with. He was as regal in his appearance as any of the Wardens, but there was anger flashing in his eyes.

"SILENCE!" the King shouted. The echoes of the bellow from within the cavern rattled inside my body. Sydney fell flat on her face in fear. The Elder-

Wardens, standing in a circle around them all, each fell backwards a step as the command reverberated on and through them. The shout went out and faded into the distance and then, as if finally finding the limits of the Warden-Realm, bounced back from afar and returned upon them with nearly the same force as when it had first gone forth. As if a wave had struck them, the Elder-Wardens, who had stumbled backwards when the command had first struck them, now stumbled forwards as it hit them again as it returned.

A moment later, coming from the deep reaches of the Warden's lair, was the hum of the Mammalites, wherever they were, no matter how far, giving their assent to the king's command: "Uh-Hummah-Hum-Hum-Hummah."

The king's counselor spoke: "It has been decided, and not another word shall be spoken."

"Uh-Hummah-Hum-Hum-Hummah," the elders said together, heads slightly down.

"Come to me, Marmor," the King ordered.

Marmor stood, and strode over to them. As he arrived, another Warden arrived—distinctly feminine, and as young as Marmor.

"Stand, Daughter of Eve," the King commanded gently. I helped Sydney to her feet. "What is your name?"

"I… my name is Sydney…" she stammered.

"That is not your name," the King replied, "but it

will do for now."

"I should think—" Sydney began, but I laughed and interrupted her.

"I'll explain later," I told her. A sound I had not heard from the Wardens before now came to my ears. It had that deep hum I was familiar with, but it now had harmonies, if not even a melody. Somehow, I knew what I was hearing was the sound of Warden-Laughter. It is my great hope and desire that all Mankind can someday hear it, even if it is at my expense.

"We shall call you Sydney," the King said. "Behold, this is Shelratha. She is young, like you, Sydney. Until we have decided how to proceed in your case, she will accompany you." With that, Shelratha laid her hand gently on Sydney's shoulder... which required Shelratha to bend down quite a bit, as with every other Warden, she towered over humans.

"Come with me, Sydney," Shelratha said.

Sydney threw a look of great concern at me but I nodded encouragingly, "It's ok, Sydney. Go with her. I know this kind, and you will be safe and have great adventures."

After Sydney was gone, the King said to me, "You should not promise such things as you cannot deliver."

"But will she not go on to assist the Wardens in their work, as I did?" I asked him.

"But she is still much younger than you were, Casey. Too young, perhaps, to do the work that you did, and too young, we fear, to keep our secrets."

"What then?" I asked.

"It has not yet been decided, as I said," the King said.

"You will send her home eventually, won't you?" I said, anger kindled.

"Have no fear, Casey, we will do what is right, but it will be done in time, not before," the King said.

"You will let her See as you have let me See, though, won't you?" I persisted.

"The less she Sees, the safer both she, and we, are," he replied.

"My King, you must let her have Sight, especially if you mean to hold her for very long. Humans are not made to be in the dark for a great length of time! You must let her have her Sight," I implored him.

The King bowed his head ever so slightly to me, "It shall be as you command, my Lord."

I knew the King didn't like when I bowed before him, but he likewise knew when he did the same to me, it made me uncomfortable. I wanted to react angrily, but I felt the laughter of the Wardens wash over and through me again, and was forced to relent.

CHAPTER 5.

Marmor led me away from the Great Cavern through the Warden's brilliantly lit tunnels. It was unfortunate that such beauty was closed off from the scrutiny of Mankind, but I understood why that was the case. I remembered again how privileged I was to see such spectacles.

"I am sorry I got you in trouble, Marmor," I said to my old friend.

"It is my fault, but as you say, had I noticed her I would have continued anyway. It was, perhaps, God's will all along. Still, I must stop bringing in threats to our realm, or I will be cast out, I suspect," he said.

"That can happen?" I said, glancing at him.

"Indeed. They are put into exile into your world, with their ability to enter our realm removed. They wander the woods and rivers of your realm alone. This is one reason why the Race of Man has any indication at all that we exist. Imagine, though, what sins one must have committed as a Warden for the King to decide it is better to be thrust into the creek beds of Mankind than to be allowed to walk free in our realm."

"What will happen with Sydney?" I asked.

"I do not know. It is not my business to know," he replied.

Struck by a new thought, "What will happen with

me?"

I sensed that Marmor was smiling. "Your adventure continues, Casey. For how long with us, I do not know. Let me tell you what I do know."

I listened, then, as Marmor told me all he knew.

He had been carrying on the work of the Wardens, opening and closing the gates of heaven so that the Ministers of Men could come to and fro and do battle, when a messenger interrupted his work with an urgent message: immediately go forth and retrieve Casey from mortal danger.

Upon hearing this, I was in the first place glad for the fact that, unlike humans, Mammalites are not the sort to sit around trying to understand *why* commands are given, but rather obey them right away. In the second place, I was floored by the fact that an angel would have any interest in me, whatsoever. "I must be mighty special," I said to myself.

Marmor continued with his tale.

"Now I am to escort you to do a task which the messenger has ordained. Once you complete your task, I am to take you back to where I plucked you from. Do not ask me why you are to do as commanded," he said.

"I know, I know," I said. "I'm sure you didn't even ask for that information. But what is the task?"

"It is almost now upon us," he said. "It is this: I will open a door for you and you will enter your world and retrieve an item. It is the tip of a spear. There is nothing special about the spearpoint. In fact, that is the point. There will be several to choose from, it makes no difference which you choose. Only choose quickly, so that I can retrieve you and escort you home."

"Sounds easy enough," I replied.

"Good, because we are here."

Marmor opened the door to the tunnel and pushed me through it, standing there between the two worlds as I took in my surroundings.

It appeared to me that I was in the armory of a medieval castle, given the fact that there was arrayed around me, hanging from the stone walls, shields, swords, and bows and arrows. In my imagination, places like this would have been coated in dust and smell, well, *old*, but it all seemed very new. A chimney was built into one side of the rock wall, and I could see that embers still glowed on the hearth. The room was lit by numerous torches, making it well-lit, allowing me to see all the items clearly.

I made my way around the room touching the different weapons with wonder and awe. There was some really cool stuff in here!

"Hurry up, Casey!" Marmor hissed at me.

Of course. All these lit torches and the glowing embers indicated this room was still very much in use, and someone could come in at any moment. I forced myself to stop gawking at the weaponry and turned about, looking for the tips of spears. Finally spotting what appeared to be the spears themselves leaning up against the wall, I let my eyes follow them to the floor, where indeed there were a large assortment of sharp points that slid over the spears and were fastened there for battle.

Standing over the tips, I saw that Marmor spoke truly when he said that there would be many to choose from. I picked up one after another in turn, inspecting them, trying to decide which one would be the neatest one to own.

"Casey!" Marmor snapped.

"Oops," I said, hearing for the first time the sound of voices in conversation drawing closer to me. The door to the armory opened as the door to the Warden-Realm closed behind me.

"Dear Casey, why did you tarry?" Marmor chided me as we once again took to the Time Tunnels.

I shrugged, and smiled, "All's well that ends well."

I looked at the spear tip in my hand. It bore the impressions of having been used in battle, but there wasn't a bit of rust on it or anything to give an indication that it was old. It made me wonder where in the world people might still be using spears as weapons. For that matter, who would be using them? Later I would realize I was asking the wrong question. I should have been asking *when* were they using them.

CHAPTER 6

I was ill-prepared for what happened when I stepped through the Warden-Gate back into my bedroom at the Estate house. Sunlight was streaming through the windows and the tranquility of the moment could have led me to believe that it was just another day of study in front of me. When I went downstairs, however, I heard a murmur of conversations coming from the grand living room. I walked into the room and took stock of what I was seeing.

There were thirty to forty people standing or sitting around the room, sipping coffee, chatting quietly together. I saw Myrtle and Mr. Chaffee. My parents, of course. My siblings, yes. Also, though, men in dark suits that looked intimidating. At each corner, and immediately to my left as I walked through the door, were men in fatigues with sidearms on their hips. As my presence became known, the conversations came to a halt. Finally, it was just my parents talking with Myrtle, and when these realized that something was afoot, they turned their gaze towards the door.

Upon catching sight of me, my mother leapt up and ran to me, calling out my name, and when reaching me she hugged me tightly and dripped hot tears on to my face. My father was hot on her heels and Myrtle and Mr. Chaffee weren't very far behind.

Everyone else was on their feet to better see what was going on.

"Ma. Ma… MA! I'm alright, Ma," I said, gently pushing her away.

Myrtle gave a nod towards the guard at the door, and he disappeared into the hallway.

"Where is Sydney?" my mom cried out.

Now it struck me what kind of a pickle I was in. When I had disappeared into the Warden-Realm the first time, I was returned at the very moment I left, and no one was the wiser. The Wardens couldn't very well do that again without putting us back into imminent danger. Still, I *was* returned. Sydney, was yet in their care! How could I assure my parents that Sydney was safe without giving away the secrets of the Wardens? It wasn't just my parents in the room, either. There were many people I didn't even know.

"She's fine, ma. Honest," I said.

"But *where* is she?" she repeated.

"Uh… completely safe…" I yammered.

"Where?" my mother insisted.

"Uh…" my eyes caught Myrtle's.

"Why don't we just excuse ourselves for a few moments?" Myrtle suggested. When my parents made to follow, she put her hand out. "Just give me and Chaffee a moment alone with Casey. Please trust us."

I left my weeping mother in the doorway with my father to console her and found an unused room to duck into. Once the door was closed, I shared with them all that had happened and all that I knew.

Mr. Chaffee filled me in on what I didn't know. "We chased the intruder through the house but he jumped through a window and fled on foot into the woods. We have yet to find him. Security, as I'm sure you have noticed, has been increased. Unfortunately, the intruder seriously injured the guard that night. He is still in critical condition at the hospital. Good reasons to think he will recover, but the docs aren't willing to commit to more than that."

"And we don't know who he was?" I asked.

"Nope. At present not even a clue. But we have our best working on it," Mr. Chaffee said.

Myrtle interrupted, "We have to decide what to tell people, especially your parents, Casey. They would never believe the truth even if we told them, but telling a lie is not an alternative, either. I could ask them again to simply trust me, and trust you, but from their point of view, all I bring to the table is a lot of money. Your father would be most offended if anything I said comes even close to suggesting that I am trying to buy his silence. Your mother will not be consoled unless she can put her hands on her daughter. And yet, telling them the truth is not an option."

"An impossible situation," I frowned.

There was a moment of silence as each of us reflected on the available choices before us.

At last, Myrtle spoke. "I need to have a 'heart to heart' with your folks, Casey. Mr. Chaffee, why don't you take Casey's souvenir to the library and secure it there, and then say whatever you think is right to disperse all of our guests. Increase the guard."

"What will you say, Myrtle?" I asked her after Mr. Chaffee left.

"I guess I'll find out soon," she laughed. "Go greet your siblings and set their minds at ease as best you can, and send your parents in."

∞ ∞ ∞

My parents were with Myrtle for a long time. I can't be sure, but I thought one time I heard my father shouting. I wanted to rush in and tell them everything, but knew better. I did my best to assure my siblings that Sydney was quite alright, but without being able to give them any particulars, it flew about as well as I'm sure it was flying with my parents.

At long last, my parents emerged. My mother had been dabbing her eyes like a boss, and it showed. My father's lips were drawn tightly together, but when he saw me, he tried to force himself to smile. Myrtle came out last, looking exhausted. She, too, when she saw me, forced herself to smile. The ageless Myrtle looked like she had aged a solid day, maybe even a day and a half.

By now, we had the place to ourselves again. The guests had all left and the guards, their numbers beefed up, stood guard around the perimeter of the house and the property in general. We tried to relax, but I could tell there was still some tension between Myrtle and my parents. Eventually, my siblings went to their rooms, and I was alone with Myrtle, Mr. Chaffee, and my parents.

My father pricked the tension, gazing hard at me as he did, saying, "It would appear, son, that we have allowed you to commit yourself to a concern that was far more dangerous than we appreciated initially. I don't know what kind of operation Myrtle is running here… to tell you the truth, I'm having trouble wrapping my head around the idea that someone as young as her could be running any kind of operation… but be that as it may, it is clear enough that it is clandestine to the extreme. She assures me that you are aware of the risks, and welcome them. Is that true?"

I collected my thoughts carefully. I wanted to give a complete and full answer, without jeopardizing the Wardens, or my parents themselves.

"I have already seen amazing things. Things that if you had seen them yourselves, you wouldn't now be asking that question. I won't tell you that I am aware of *all* the risks, because I have a lot to learn. That said, not just Myrtle, but you yourself, have been trying to train me for the dangers of the real world. I have reasons to think that I can be very useful. I want you to know that Sydney has now also seen some amazing things. She cannot be in safer hands, either. I'd trust all these people with my life and hers, too. If you had the opportunity, you would too. But... I can't tell you more than that... it might bring about dangers that can't exist at all as long as I don't talk about them."

"Well, that is as clear as mud," my mother frowned.

"It is clear enough, I suppose," my dad said. He turned his attention now to Myrtle and Mr. Chaffee. "I have appreciated what you have done for my family and certainly what you have done with Casey. It is quite the 'ask' to trust you about Sydney, but Casey has never been one to lie. As hard as it is, we're going to proceed on that basis, although we'll need some help along the way. But I do have one request... more of a demand, actually..."

"Go ahead," Myrtle said.

My father continued, "Well, you've been stuffing the kid full of knowledge and information, but if he's actually going to be put in danger, you've got to give him some skills. He has to learn how to fight. He needs to know how to defend himself. I mean, he needs the training of a soldier. Not training like a soldier, the training *of a soldier*. It just wouldn't be right to put him in danger, even if he volunteers for it, if he doesn't have that kind of preparation."

My mother shifted in her seat. She didn't like this kind of talk, and it was clear my father had not discussed this with her.

Mr. Chaffee stood up from his own seat and strode over to my father who instinctively stood up to face him. Mr. Chaffee put his hand out, and my father took it. Mr. Chaffee clasped my father's hand tightly and he looked him in the eye and declared, "You don't just have my word on it; I pledge my life to it."

They stood like that for a lingering moment, man to man, eye to eye, grip in grip. Then, Mr. Chaffee knelt before my mother and took her hand (just one, because the other was dabbing hard at her cheeks) and said, "I will train him myself, and vow to lay down my own life if necessary to protect Casey's."

My mom bawled.

"Ma… mom…" I said, shaking my head. It hurt to see her so sad, but knowing that she was crying over what I knew was presently a rather benign situation made it even harder to bear.

Without receiving an answer from her, Mr. Chaffee got up and now walked over to me. He put his hand on my shoulder and said, loud enough for all to hear, "Your training begins tomorrow."

Then Mr. Chaffee left the room.

This seemed to end the matter for everyone, and not another word was said about it. Myrtle excused herself. My mother re-gained her composure. As the evening turned into night, I chatted with them and my siblings, trying (rather successfully, in my opinion) to avoid any matters of controversy.

Everyone went to bed and the night passed without incident.

In the morning, I said my goodbyes to my family, and that very day Mr. Chaffee began the training he had promised.

CHAPTER 7.

Mr. Chaffee took the training seriously. At first, I was excited about it. One week later, I was wishing foul things would happen to the man. Mr. Chaffee was taking the training *too* seriously, I concluded, as hatred for him began to boil in me. Training in the morning, training in the day time, training at night. Sometimes, training at 3 a.m. Push-ups, running, weight-lifting. Some days I would get lucky and we would ease up on the calisthenics and I would receive weapons training. Assemble the gun. Field strip it. Put it back together. Take it apart. Assemble it. Over and over and over and over again. Then more running. More push-ups. Sit-ups. Grappling. Hand to hand combat, with Mr. Chaffee kicking my tail over and over and over and over again.

After about a month of this, I noticed something strange when I looked in the mirror. I appeared to have muscles.

"Where did those come from?" I wondered. They seemed to have arrived overnight. I decided I liked having them more than not having them, and my fury at being worked so hard by 'Mr. *Chafe*' began to cool.

As for Mr. Chaffee, he had to have known that for a time I wanted nothing more than to pummel his face forever, but he never changed his expression or his approach.

Meanwhile, I was still expected to use the 'off' hours to study. A certain Dr. Kem visited every other day for a few hours to add further insights into whatever it was I was reading. Once a week he would give a one-on-one lecture about some matter, usually related to something scientific.

The whole regime was exhausting, but I found also that the stronger I got, the more I could bear both the physical and intellectual adversities I was undergoing. Then there was a curve ball thrown at me.

About three months into the training, two men arrived. One was named Jessup Patterson. He hated his first name, so he went by his last name, which was often shortened simply to 'Pat.' He was a little taller than me, with long black hair that was tied up in a pony tail. He was just a little older than me. It was soon very clear that he had been part of Myrtle's organization for quite a few years. The second was named Colin Randall. He was quite a bit older than me, but still in his twenties. I quickly learned that he was in the military. He was coy about what he actually did and what branch he served in, but he was built like a brick.

Colin took over the training at that point and Patterson became my work-out partner. Because Patterson had already been in training for a while and was a little older than me, not to mention bigger than me, I went from being merely physically exhausted to actually beaten. I was pummeled every day and still had to do my studies. Once again, hatred began to grow in my belly.

About a month after that, though, I looked in the mirror and saw even *more* muscles. I had muscles on top of muscles. There was *definition*. I decided the beatings were bearing fruit, and let the anger dissipate from my body.

By the fifth month, I started to hold my own. I mean, relatively speaking. Patterson's bigger size gave him a natural advantage and there was no way I could make myself grow in that sense. I would just have to wait for my body to do its thing. But I knew things were changing when I'd hear Patterson grunt as he tried, and failed, to work me over, saying things like, "You're a scrapper, Casey. A real scrapper." Colin looked on, grinning.

Just as I was really starting to get into my groove, Colin changed up the training. There was a lot more emphasis on weaponry skills added to the daily regime. He made sure I could shoot straight and true by increasing the distances at the target range. There were a half dozen excursions into nearby forests to practice survival skills and tactics useful for moving undetected through vegetation. Then we did the same thing, but in urban settings.

It was somewhere in here that Mr. Chaffee told me that my training would be winding down, and we were finally going to go on that trip that I was supposed to go on before I was attacked in my sleep. First, however, he had a real treat for me: I was to learn how to use weapons and equipment from the past. "After all," he told me, "Given your experiences, you may very well find yourself in a time and place where only swords are available."

The time for training on ancient weapons finally came. Colin wrapped up his lessons for me and Patterson, and now the master was to become the student. Mr. Chaffee had invited another expert to the estate to teach us all how to use swords and other weapons from the past, and Colin was to learn as well.

"My name is Jorge," the BladeMaster said. He had long blond hair that he had to keep pushing away from his eyes. He wore a loose-fitting shirt and a leather vest, but you could tell just by looking at him that he was well-muscled, even if not very bulky. He whirled a sword around expertly, blowing wind our way, and growled at us, "They are paying me big money to teach you how to fight with the weapons of the past. I trust that you will give me your undivided attention."

He need not have asked. The three of us enthusiastically took to the lessons. It wasn't all swordplay, as there were many weapons in use besides those that used gunpowder. He brought us up to speed with the bow and arrow and the crossbow, too. We learned how to fight with a staff as well as a simple club. Eventually we figured out that before the advent of 'the great equalizer' just about any object could be made into a weapon, although obviously in war we would prefer the staples of warfare: the sword, the lance, the bow and arrow.

To cap it all off, Jorge then arranged to have horses brought to the estate, and he taught us how to ride them. After we learned how to ride them, he taught us how to *fight* on them. Of the three of us, it is fair to say that only Colin was competent enough to ride into battle with a sword, but that didn't mean that Patterson and I weren't dangerous.

In my young life to that point, I had already experienced many great things, but that nine months was probably the coolest of all of them. If you ever have a chance to participate in a program like that, I *strongly* recommend it.

Granted, there was never any thought that I would actually have to go to war. Both Colin and Mr. Chaffee said more than once that I was learning these skills for a reason, and I should bear that reason in mind. If I thought then that I would ever have to really use the skills, I suppose I would have felt differently about it. In fact, in that circumstance, I might go further and consider removing my recommendation—except, in that circumstance, you would be very happy, indeed, you had received some training.

"Mighty fine work, lads," Jorge said. His time with us was coming to an end and there was one last session planned. "Before we part ways, we're going to do a little sparring!"

Now, there were few things that I enjoyed more than sparring. Nine months ago, not so much. But today? I couldn't get enough. I looked at Colin and Patterson and they looked at me, pleased as punch.

"You ready to throw down?" Patterson asked, grabbing a staff from where it lay on the weapons table.

I grabbed the wooden broadsword, "I'm making sure you come with me if I do."

Colin chuckled as he mulled over which weapon to use. He decided to go with the ball and chain, which, fortunately, was only a heavy foam ball attached to thick rope. It wouldn't kill you, but it would hurt like the dickens.

We stood facing each other on the green, waiting for the go-ahead.

"Lads, lads, lads!" Jorge laughed, taking off his vest, and then the shirt. "No, lads, it's all three of *you* against *me*, all at once!"

Our grins slowly faded as more of Jorge's torso became visible. It was criss-crossed with scars of all shapes and sizes. There were the signs of sword-slashes, the marks of being punctured (or shot, I reckon), but most ominous of all were the several thick scars that encircled his entire neck—at least three of them, as near as I could tell.

"Ho boy, we're in for it, fellahs," Colin whispered.

Jorge turned to face us, cracked his knuckles, and grinned. "Shall we dance?" he smirked.

A mere instant after we nodded, Jorge was upon us, kicking and punching. We, of course, were wearing pads and a helmet, but Jorge was not. Getting hit with any of our chosen weapons hurt, pads or no pads, but the terms of engagement mitigated against serious harm. Jorge had not bothered to tell us the terms of engagement, but we instinctively fought less aggressively than we would have had Jorge been wearing protective gear. This all started to go out the window as it became clear that Jorge had no interest in pulling *his* punches.

The first to turn the dial all the way up was Patterson. Jorge stepped on my sword, punched Colin in the gut, and then grabbed hold of Pat's pony tail with both hands and dove to the dirt, bringing Pat's head with him. Pat dropped his staff well into the descent but picked it up as soon as he could regain his feet. He was furious, and pulled no more punches.

The problem, of course, was that one was always trying not to strike an ally, whereas Jorge didn't have any such concerns. All this time, we had been training to fight alone, but had never once fought together. It showed. Meanwhile, Jorge danced around, poking us in the face, stomping on our feet, and smacking us in our rumps. Not that we didn't land a few blows here and there! After just a few minutes, all four of us were bleeding, *somewhere*.

This battle royale was going nowhere, fast, when I had myself a bright idea: "Let's lose the weapons guys. Just grab him!"

We each tossed aside our weapons and lunged for him. Naturally, Jorge grabbed the staff and gave us each one good whack, cackling as he did so. Only one good whack, though, because by then the three of us were on him, kicking, scratching, punching, yanking.

Now, it is hard to explain, but you can always tell when you've been defeated, and the other person usually knows it, too. Jorge managed to get a 'kill' shot on Colin, first, then one on the still enraged Patterson. Jorge and I continued to battle for a few more minutes, most of which I spent on defense, until finally I, too, succumbed.

We all lay there on our backs in the grass, wheezing. Jorge was laughing. Eventually we were all laughing.

"I can't believe you pulled my hair," Patterson said.

"I've got hair, too," Jorge replied. "Why didn't you pull it?"

"I tried, man, I tried. I tell you I tried!" Patterson laughed.

After a long while, we all got up and limped back

into the estate to shower and recuperate. Jorge announced that training was over. We had passed with flying colors.

The three of them departed, each in turn, over the next few days, leaving me alone at the estate again. I was given the impression that I was finally going to be permitted to more formally join the ranks of those active in Myrtle's organization. I was now closer to sixteen than fifteen, and I knew from my studies that historically speaking, there were plenty of people who were regarded as adults by that age, often because they were thrust into it by necessity. Would Myrtle and Mr. Chaffee deem me ready?

Finally, a night arrived when I was given a message telling me I could expect Myrtle to arrive the next day. With a little anxiety mixed in, I was looking forward to her verdict.

CHAPTER 8.

The estate was buzzing with activity long before I woke up the next morning. Myrtle had indeed arrived, and with her a large contingent of armed guards, and a fair number of people who belonged to her organization doing duties I did not know. I could hear them all from my bedroom so I made sure to be ready for polite company before I joined them. It was so busy that no one even noticed me. I helped myself to a breakfast roll and wandered into the library hoping that there, at least, would be peace.

Nope. I interrupted a meeting in progress.

"Ah," said Myrtle, beaming so brightly she may as well have been a second sun. She continued, "Allow me to introduce you all to our newest companion, Casey."

I wiped a crumb off my cheek and tried not to blush. I mumbled something in reply... my mouth was full, so mumbling was all I could do.

"Come and sit," she said, directing me to an open chair. She then continued holding forth around a large conference room-sized table that had numerous people sitting around it that I had never seen before. When my eyes finally found Mr. Chaffee's he nodded at me, and I nodded in return.

"And so," Myrtle was concluding, "in that contingency, you all know what to do. We all hope and pray that it won't happen, but we must at least consider the possibility. You are dismissed."

The people slowly got up and gathered their things, talking amongst themselves, and gradually left the room until the only ones left were me, Mr. Chaffee, and Myrtle.

"What is this all about?" I asked.

"There is quite an adventure ahead of us," Myrtle laughed.

Mr. Chaffee picked up the thread, "There is a chance that we will all be gone for a long while, so it was necessary to make sure everyone knew what to do while we were gone…"

Myrtle cut him off, "Let us not speak in euphemisms, dear man. Casey may be going with us, so he may as well hear it put directly."

"Hear what, exactly?" I asked.

Myrtle came round so that she stood in front of me and put her hands on my shoulders. Looking me directly in the eyes—my knees wobbled as I saw within them the cascading purple waves of a storm at sea—she said, "We might not come back at all. In fact, we may all be going right to our deaths!" She seemed happy as she said it, as if there was nothing that could bring her greater joy. Standing in her majestic presence I almost felt the same way, but it was a mirth that washed over me rather than welled up within me. It was Myrtle's Mirth: irresistible, unfathomable—and what all people would have possessed at every moment of every day forever and ever if only Adam and Eve had not blackened humanity's fate with one despicable act.

"Um, well, good to … get things in order, then," I stammered.

"In that spirit, there is something that you have to get in order, too. If you come with us, you may be dead this time tomorrow. I want you to think upon that fact very carefully. If you still want to go forward, I have arranged to have you visit your family this very evening. Obviously, you can't tell them it might be the last time you are together. But it is only right that you are with them," Myrtle explained.

"Well, this seems rather… serious. When I signed on to this, I knew there were risks. Is there anything in particular about this mission that makes it more risky?" I asked.

Mr. Chaffee shook his head, "We cannot tell you the details, lest you inadvertently say something you shouldn't with your family. Even then, however, the truth is there isn't much to say. This mission comes from up high."

"Up high?" I asked.

Myrtle pointed to the sky.

"The Big Guy?" I gasped.

"Well, the message was delivered by a Mammalite, so, close enough," Myrtle laughed.

"I don't see how I could turn down Him!" I said.

"Dear Casey, that's noble!" Myrtle said, taking my

hand in hers. "But only *I* have been commanded to go on this mission. You and Mr. Chaffee have *the option*. You can each choose not to, and no one, not even 'The Big Guy,' will hold it against you."

"Well, I'm going," I declared. "So, enough of this 'choosing not to' business!"

Mr. Chaffee grinned at me and Myrtle smiled.

"Very well," Myrtle said. "This evening, you dine with your parents. Tomorrow morning you will wake early. We will share with you the details of the mission, such as we know them. I am told that our old friend Marmor will be coming to take us."

"Mr. Chaffee too?" I asked, excited. As far as I knew, while Mr. Chaffee knew about the Mammalites and the time tunnels, he had never seen them himself.

"When I heard the details of the mission…" he began, but Myrtle cut him off.

"It waits until tomorrow," she ordered.

And that was that.

∞ ∞ ∞

I spent a glorious evening with my family that night. They had been told I was going on a trip (which was true) and that I could be gone a very long time (also, technically true), so they pulled out all the stops to entertain me. All my favorite foods and drinks were there. Even Tom, my oldest brother, who had been in college this whole time, came to see me off.

I fared far better in the rough-housing out on the lawn than I ever had before, impressing my brothers tremendously, and puffing up my ego considerably.

"Maybe it's just me," my mom said to my dad as we were coming back into the house, "but Casey seems rather... *built*."

My dad smiled. "It's good to know Myrtle and Chaffee keep their word." Later that evening, I told them a little about all the training that I had received the last year. Naturally, I left out details such as 'hey, you might have to fight with a sword some day!'

They asked me about Sydney, which was by far the lowest note of the night. I had to tell them the same thing I said before: she was safe, secure, and undoubtedly the happiest she'd ever been. Apart from that, I had nothing to add. Jessica hung on my every word.

Eventually, the good times ended. A driver came to fetch me back to the estate. It was alright. I missed my family and enjoyed their company, but I was ready for adventure. I felt as though I had never been more ready. It would be a waste of my skills if all I did was sit in a library the rest of my life—or so I told myself. At any rate, when my head hit the pillow, I wasn't thinking at all about the possibility that it might be the last time I slept in a bed. I was thinking only of waking up and getting on with things.

CHAPTER 9.

I clutched the spearhead in my hand so tightly I could feel the edges start to bite into my palm. I didn't dare loosen my grip. If I lost it now, after having already gone through so much, that pain would have been far greater than cuts on my hand. And where was Myrtle and Mr. Chaffee? Dead, I feared. Things weren't looking so great for me, either.

The shouting from all sides made my heart race. I had seen my share of war movies and read plenty of first-hand accounts of ancient battles, but none prepared me for the horror I was presently wading through.

∞ ∞ ∞

It had all started well enough. That's the way it always is when you are trotting along after Marmor in one of the crystal hallways of the Wardens. There was an additional warm overtone to the journey because this time I took it with Myrtle and Mr. Chaffee. It was fun to watch Mr. Chaffee's expression as he saw for the first time the glories that Myrtle and I had seen in our time in the Warden-Realm.

I wasn't the least bit anxious, either. First of all, I remembered well the reception the Wardens gave when they deposited Myrtle next to me in Jerusalem, in my first great adventure with Myrtle. The hosts of heaven gushed out over the plains to guard their charge before moving on to do their various duties at that portentous moment. What could be feared with that kind of advance guard blazing away?

It wasn't as if I hadn't been warned. While the mission itself was simple enough, Mr. Chaffee made it perfectly clear that the theater of operations we were going to be dropping into would be dripping with imminent danger and surrounded by maximum bloodshed.

The mission? Find the Lance of Longinus. Find it, and swap it with the spear-tip I had stolen from a medieval castle nearly a year before, and make sure no one saw me do it. This spear-tip was the very same that the Roman soldier Longinus plunged into Jesus' side as he hung on the cross, releasing blood and water from the wound to the amazement of all, Longinus included.

Presumably, Jesus' blood was still on the tip, making it just the sort of thing that Draco would be angling for. There had been many claims over the centuries that this tip or that one was the 'real' one, but of course nobody had access to the kind of authoritative information that Myrtle did, whether through her organization of spies, or her close collaboration with the Wardens, who moved in and out of our time as easily as you and I can walk through a door.

It so happened that this information led to the conclusion that the lance that was reported discovered by a certain Peter Bartholomew in the early summer of 1098 A.D. in Antioch was the *real* lance. Fortunately, the date of that discovery was something that could be worked out with a high level of accuracy, which made it practical to arrive at just the right time.

Unfortunately, the discovery of the lance was made at the height of the Siege of Antioch in the First Crusade. The city was swarming with thousands of combatants as the battle ebbed and flowed. One day, the Crusaders lay siege to the Seljuk Turks. The next day, the Crusaders were in the city, laying waste to it. The day after *that*, more Muslims arrived, this time from as far away as Persia, and they laid siege to the Crusaders!

It was during this time and at that place that I was sent. The timing was both perfect and terrible, at the same time.

Almost immediately, I was separated from Myrtle and Mr. Chaffee. That had not been part of the plan, but the chaos was intense and immediate. The Crusaders were busy executing the city's residents, who were fleeing for their lives: Christian or Muslim, the Crusaders spared none. I had to hide among the dead bodies to avoid being chopped to death, myself.

"The next time Myrtle says a mission might kill me, I'm going to have to take it much more seriously," I said to myself as I creeped along the ancient city in the dead of night. Antioch was ancient even then—well over a thousand years old.

Before they left on the journey, they had a fairly extensive briefing about the mission. Thanks to this, I had a decent understanding of the layout of the city. I had a general notion about what groups of people were doing what, when, and where, although this was based on witness accounts which were often muddy. I knew I had a limited window of time to locate the spearhead before it would be in the wind. In the present day, the Lance presumably resided in the Vatican. However, over those centuries there would have been ample time and opportunity for Draco to get a hold of it, and this was the best chance we had to make sure that what he actually touched was the 'fake' I was now clinging to so tightly.

What made matters worse was that my education had not yet given me a background in foreign languages. Numerous languages were spoken in Antioch at this time. Granted, even the people I was sure were speaking English sounded foreign to me! I had to use all my wits to discern what was happening around me not only to figure out when and where my next best opportunity was to make the switch, but also to simply stay alive.

I did some math in my head. "I reckon I arrived on June 3rd. I've been slinking about for two days.

Bartholomew is going to find that thing on the 15th. I've got ten days to find the cathedral of Saint Peter and find the Lance before the Crusaders do… that's a long time… why did we come so early?"

But as the days went by, I started to appreciate why I needed the extra time. For one thing, it took an excruciatingly long time to move through the city undetected. One night, I was only able to go one block. I slept during the days. At this point, Kerbogha and his army had the city surrounded and there were constant points of friction along the city walls, necessitating rapid responses by the Crusaders. Thus, at any moment, a large contingent of Crusaders could come charging through my alley. Then, when I finally arrived at the cathedral—on the 11th, I think—I discovered that it was in constant use by the Crusaders. I couldn't just head to the basement and start digging! I had to wait for the coast to be clear, and remain hidden in the meantime.

After several nights of trying to pull off my own amateur archeological dig without anyone noticing, I realized it was a lost cause.

I knew that the records indicated that the Crusaders had dug a pit and Bartholomew 'magically' discovered the Lance at the bottom of it, after everyone else had failed to find it. Personally, I believed ol' Bart had it all along, perhaps discovered in a secret place in the cathedral.

My thinking was that once the Crusaders gained access to the cathedral, wresting Antioch from the Turks, Bartholomew was one of the first to get to the cathedral. I believed he went there looking for the Lance right from the start, found it, and then waited for the right moment to produce it.

During our briefing before we left on the mission, the three of us debated this point. The hitch was that Bartholomew had been claiming to have visions about the Lance long before the Crusaders took the city. Perhaps he really was receiving visions. Perhaps he had good reason to believe the Lance was in the cathedral before they took Antioch. One thing seemed certain: Bartholomew genuinely believed he had the real Lance. Since we had the benefit of reading the historical records, we knew he staked his life on the claim it was the real Lance—something he would not have done if he knew definitively that the Lance was a fake, because *he* had faked it.

People won't die for a lie if they know it's a lie.

All that said, I couldn't believe that the Lance was something that would have been buried. Still, I had to look.

My back-up plan was to be there as Bartholomew and the Crusaders finally arrived and took over the 'dig.' I reasoned that if I could get close enough, I could make the swap without anyone being the wiser. Thinking that Bartholomew had the spear in his pocket the whole time, when the moment arrived, I tried to get close enough to dip my hand into his pocket and replace the real Lance with my spear-tip. Sadly, there were far too many people around. As subtle as I had learned to be, there was nothing I could do but watch ol' Bart ascend triumphantly from the pit with the Lance held high above his head, vindicated.

I continued to shadow the Lance as best I could for the next couple of days, but it didn't take long before I lost track of it.

"Well," I said to myself, chewing a piece of moldy bread and trying on the boot of a dead Crusader, "Ol' Ray of Aguil-sumthin is going to be surprising Kerbogha on the 28th. He'll be riding out of this town on a valiant charge with the Lance leading the way." I peeked my head into the alley. I thought I had heard something. Seeing nothing, I pulled back into the abandoned stone abode, and continued my munching and my ruminations.

"He led that charge from the Bridge Gate... It is the 25th today. What is that... a mile away?" I crunched the bread. Man, was I hungry. "I can do that in three days. Easy." Crunch-crunch. "I gotta start tonight, though."

I also figured I was more likely to find Myrtle and Chaffee (assuming they were still alive) by being on the move rather than just hiding in a hole. Plan in hand, I set out at once, using the cover of night to conceal my movements.

It was tough going the next couple of days. The Crusaders exhibited new energy, with morale up due to the discovery of the Lance. They were gearing up for a surprise attack on the surrounding armies. Their idea was to sally forth out of the city and surprise the enemy. Fortunately for me, they were fasting in anticipation of their daring mission, which meant that nobody else was scrounging for food in the city. Unfortunately for me, dead bodies still clogged the town, and finding food was a miserable chore. It was hard enough to move through the grisly scene, let alone scavenge, so finally I decided that if the Crusaders could give up food for a few days, I could do the same.

At last, I reached my destination: halfway between the Bridge Gate and St. George's Gate. I was clad with the remnants of Crusader garments and armor that I had found lying about. In the morning, I would slip into the muster of soldiers and knights, with no one the wiser. As they rushed upon the Seljuk army in ambush, I would be with them. I was so scared, I thought I wouldn't be able to sleep a wink, but I was wrong. I was out like a light, waking only because of the clanking of the great Crusader assembly before the sun had thrown its first ray over the horizon.

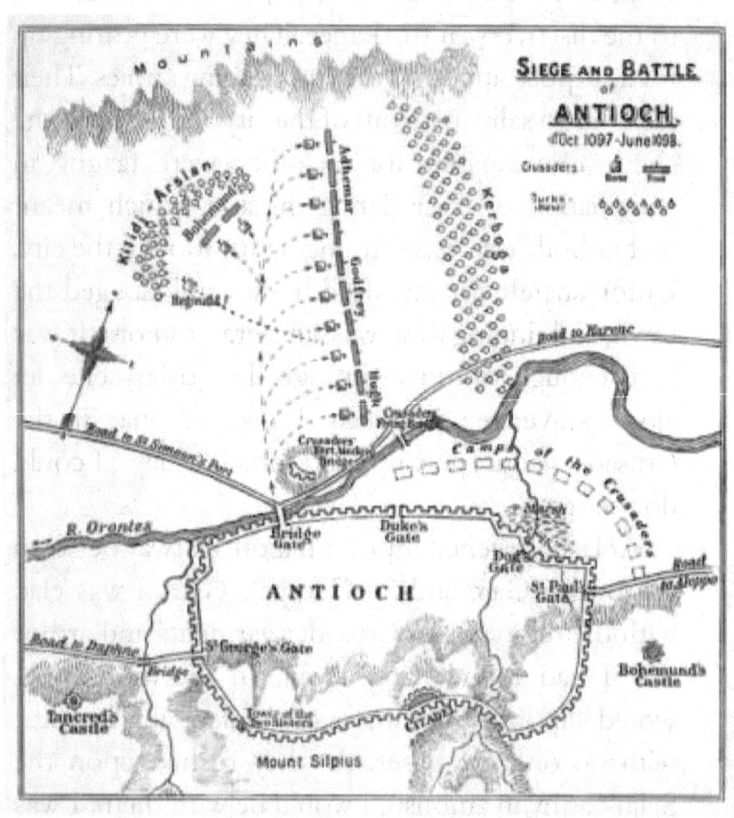

A History of the Art of War: The Middle Ages From the Fourth to the Fourteenth Century by Charles Oman, 1898.

CHAPTER 10.

Standing there, shoulder to shoulder with men from all over Medieval Europe, I couldn't help but draw energy from the electric anticipation that charged through us. Their cause was not my cause, but my life would be at risk as much as theirs. They slapped each other on the back in encouragement, and they slapped my back, as well. As if by instinct, I returned the favor. I didn't have to worry that my speech would give me away, since they made hardly a sound. These were battle-hardened soldiers—something that would be a major factor in the Crusader success that day. The ones laying siege around them had not been in constant battle for months and months like the Crusaders had. But of course, their success in their mission did not mean I would have success in mine.

The sun now lit the plains outside the city, and the horns signaled it was time. At first, it seemed as though nothing was happening. I knew, however, that it would take a few minutes to open the Bridge Gate and then some time for the great mass of us to funnel through. At last, I was marching, marching, marching. I crossed over the bridge with my comrades. I craned my head, looking for the person I knew had the Lance: Raymond of Aguilers.

In the excitement, it was hard to keep in mind the details of the battle that I had learned by study prior to coming on the mission. Assuming the records were accurate, we had a good idea of what squad was doing what, on both sides of the battle, and at what time. Recalling these details with arrows raining down on your head and men shouting, slashing, and stabbing, was an entirely different matter!

I did know, however, that Raymond was near the front line. I would have to risk all to maneuver into position close to him. I had no plan for how I was going to take the Lance from him. It occurred to me in a flash that I might have fared better if I had tried to take it back at the cathedral rather than now, in the confusion of battle. There was no time to dwell on that thought now, and, at any rate, that might not have gone well, either.

I was now within the front line, practically in the melee myself. Arrows thudded into the ground around me and thudded as often into the Crusaders near me. Swords were flashing, spears were jabbing, shields were clanging. I parried a blow from a Turk that had been part of a surging counter-attack but he was not there to receive my returning slash, as he was pushed along by his own surging companions. Seeing an opportunity, I fell in behind the surge as if following in the wake of a ship, suspecting that they might be headed towards Raymond.

In the chaos, it is hard to say if that supposition was correct, because the surge dissipated fairly quickly, but it did at least bring me within sight of

Raymond.

Raymond of Aguilers was not a soldier, he was basically a priest, effectively serving as a chaplain to the Crusaders. He was out near the front because he had the Lance, and this was the lightning rod the Crusaders were drawn to, but I understood that my purpose in this place was not to go hand to hand in combat with the Seljuks. A plan began to form in my mind.

According to the historical record, the Seljuks would withdraw, attempting to draw the Crusaders into a trap. This would backfire, because word about the great size of the Crusader attack would come to their leader, Kerbogha, too late. Thus, I knew that at some point the fog of battle would clear up, and it would be impossible to attack... yes, attack Raymond of Aguilers! I had to do it while the two great armies were intermingled, or I would never get away with it.

I shouldered my way through to where Raymond was. There was a protective circle of soldiers around him, but it wasn't very large, and it wasn't very sure. More than once, Seljuks penetrated the circle, not knowing, of course, that within it lay the catalyst of their defeat. If they had only known what had so fired up the Crusaders, I would not be the only one focusing on him. However, they did not know about the Lance. The Seljuks only knew that the Crusaders were fighting with renewed vigor. Arrows continued to fall around me. I had to act fast, or not just this moment, but my life, might be lost!

Just as another batch of Seljuks pressed in on the circle from the front, I knifed through the soldiers protecting Raymond from behind, and barreled into his back, sending him toppling to the ground. We wrestled there on the ground, his eyes wide open in fear and anger. He quickly figured out that I wasn't going for the kill, but for the Lance. I straddled him so he couldn't wiggle away. Our hands did war with each other as I sought to pry his fingers off of it.

The battle continued to rage above us and around us. Soon, he would collect his wits, and begin shouting for help. There was nothing for it: I had to strike him. Releasing my left hand from the duty of securing his wrist, I punched him hard in the face. Once was all I needed. Distracted by the pain, his grip on the Lance loosened, and he instinctively put both his hands up to his face.

At just that moment, a barrage of blows began to fall on my back and the back of my head. I rolled off of Raymond and threw my shield up to protect myself. A Crusader was trying to grab the Lance back from me! A three-way scrum materialized as Raymond, the Crusader, and myself fought for the Lance. As this battle within a battle raged, it occurred to both Raymond and myself, at roughly the same moment, that this Crusader was trying to *steal* the Lance, just as I was!

My eyes locked with the eyes of the Crusader. Somehow I knew, without knowing how, that this was another interloper of the battle. If it wasn't Draco himself, it was one of his agents. I didn't know what Draco looked like, except that I bore some resemblance to him. Even so, with blood and mud and caked on dust coating everything, it was only his eyes that unmistakably communicated. Now, I had tried not to inflict real harm on Raymond, but this attacker had no such compunction. He tried to stab or strike each of us in turn, forcing Raymond and I to create an *ad hoc* alliance on the fly, with no words exchanged.

Meanwhile the flesh of warriors above and around us fell about, some slain, some wounded, some thrusting forward on the attack, and others retreating over us as we lay on the ground, tumbling about in a vicious ball. I did perceive, however, that there was a trend to the shift: the Seljuks were advancing over us! The three of us each recognized our new danger at more or less the same time. There was now as much a chance that a Turk might run us through as that we might kill each other! In fact, although I did not know what the words meant, I could tell from the shouts around me issued by the nearby Crusaders that there was sudden, grave concern that they were losing the field.

If not for the adrenalin jolting through me, I would have been struck dead by fear.

Probably all three of us were re-thinking our situation when a murmur from the Crusader lines turned into a great roar. We each tried to glance towards the mighty sound while dodging blows and ripping at each other's hands for possession of the Lance. Soon, the roar was itself drowned out by the thudding of horses. This was good news for the Crusaders, but not so good news for the three of us, who now had to worry about being trampled to death, to boot.

Now, my task was not merely to steal the Lance, but to make a switch. All that was necessary was to remove the Lance from Raymond, replace the head of the one he had with the one I had in my pocket, and then make my getaway. With my life newly threatened, I redoubled my efforts to do this. I didn't care if Draco's soldier got a hold of the fake spearpoint. There could be some advantage to that, in fact.

Using my body to shield my actions, I fished my spearpoint from my pocket. Then, frantically, surrounded by peril on all sides, from threats both near and far, I wrested the Lance away from Raymond once again (as I had secured it several times before, only to have it taken away from me), and pressed the fake one into his hand. I was certain that neither he nor Draco's man saw me do it. It was time to get away.

I rolled away from the scrum and crawled to an

opening where I could stand up and start threading my way out of the mass of mayhem. Neither of the two men made any attempt to follow me, confirming that they did not know that a swap had been made. But I was still in grave danger. It was at that moment that the source of the change in the tide of the battle manifested itself.

I looked, and behold, a great host of white horses with knights astride them were barreling towards me. Some had lances, others had swords. Seljuks bounced off of their cavalry charge like birds hitting a window. Nearby Crusaders were shouting in jubilation, and I began to make out some of the words they were saying. Just then, a Seljuk cut me in the right arm.

I fell to the ground in pain and surprise. Seeing a shield laying there, I grabbed it and used it to deflect the swing of the Turk's next blow. My wound was not significant, but it certainly hurt! I would not last long if I was forced to fight with my left hand. I thought I was lost, when the Seljuk looked up suddenly, and turned on his heels and retreated. The Crusaders were shouting names I recognized: "Saint George! Saint Mercurius! Saint Demetrius! Saint Theodore!" Louder and louder they shouted and then their blazing white horses were upon me, too.

The rest of the dazzling cavalry continued to fly into the retreating Seljuk army but the four horses of the saints stopped near me. One of them, evidently having witnessed my most recent ordeal, trotted a few feet in my direction. He spoke to me in words I did not understand. I wanted to thank him, but as I didn't know his language in order to reply, I instead gave the sign language gesture for 'thank you.' This seemed to convey the meaning well enough.

He dismounted from his giant horse and extended a hand. I used my left hand to clasp the offered hand, and he pulled me to my feet. He held my hand firmly and looked me in the eyes. I nodded to show my gratitude. All about me, the Crusaders were crushing in on us, crying out as they did the names of the saints, and specifically calling the one that lifted me up, Saint George.

All four of these saints were supposed to have been dead for centuries. I remembered in the historical records their arrival was hailed as one of the reasons for the victory in the battle. When I read the accounts, I chalked it up to myth-making or propaganda. Despite being face to face with evidence that Myth could be Fact, I wasn't going to re-think the Crusader claims at the moment. I was just glad to be alive and eager to make my escape.

Saint George squeezed my hand tightly, his young face showing genuine concern for me, again. He did not seem any older than I was, but I saw on his hands and neck the scars from battles past. He was as much a veteran of war as any of the Crusaders around me were, that was for sure.

After what seemed like forever, Saint George released me, and the battle surged in the direction of the Seljuk lines, the saints and their cohort leading the way. I used the thinning ranks as my chance to get away. Having no idea what I should do or where I should go now that I had the Lance, I did the only thing that seemed to make sense: I made my way to Saint George's gate, and there tended to my wound.

Before I fell asleep, I thought about what had just transpired. I thought about Saint George's stout grip as he lifted me from the ground, and his earnest eyes peering into mine, to sense if I was well. I didn't know if it was really Saint George, but I did know this: I had seen those eyes before.

CHAPTER 11.

"Wake up, Casey," Sydney said, in a soothing, sing-song tone.

My eyelids lifted, and I knew at once that I was in the Warden-Realm. It surprised me that I needed Sydney to wake me at all, as I woke up completely refreshed, without any stupor at all. My body was cooled by the stone slab I was laying on. I needed no blanket; I was completely comfortable. I sat up and looked at my arm.

"Well, look at that!" I said. It was perfectly healed.

Marmor was entering the gleaming cavern at just that moment and I gave him the appropriate greeting. Then I asked the obvious question, "How have I come to be healed so fast?"

He smiled, "The marvelous medicines of the Wardens and the powerful healing power of your own, exquisitely designed body combined to make you whole. And, at any rate, it was just a flesh wound!"

"Quite the flesh wound," I said. There was a scar five inches long scratched in a diagonal from the upper tricep to the lower bicep. I recalled well that it was deep enough to smart. It could have been worse, but a centimeter-deep cut was no trifling matter. But it was over now. I was truly fortunate to have such friends! "And how did I come to this place?"

"I fetched, you of course," Marmor said. "Your

mission in Antioch was a success. There is one small chore left, and then the matter will be behind you. For now, though, speak with your sister. She has missed you greatly!" And with that, he excused himself.

Sydney slipped her hand into mine in and leaned her head on my shoulder. I was taken back by the display of affection but ready to reciprocate. I guess absence does make the heart grow fonder.

I also couldn't help but notice that she appeared to have aged a couple of years. This surprised me, because I knew that time proceeded differently in the Mammalite's lair. After my time there, I was returned to my family and it was as if I had never left.

"If I didn't know better, Sydney, you've had a birthday or two," I said. "How are things going for you with the Wardens?"

She blushed. "They don't want me to tell you," she said.

"Surprising but not surprising, I guess. Did they tell you why?" I asked.

"Because I was so young they were afraid I would speak too freely about what I had seen. So, I've been spending some time... here... It has been a wonderful time. But, of course I miss everyone. They said that my *not* telling you about how I've spent my time would help prove I was ready to go home," she explained.

"That sounds like them," I laughed.

She continued, "They said it's like 'faith.' About how it's not a blind commitment to a person or idea, but instead it's based on how people keep their little promises, over and over again, and are so reliable that when they finally come to a big promise, you know that they'll keep that one, too."

"Alright," I said. "Kind of like how God kept his promises throughout the Bible, and when he kept his promise to come as a man, he promised he wouldn't just die and rise again, but also would return. He did all the other things, so we know he'll do this big thing, when he is good and ready. Makes sense to me. So, in this case, you promised not to tell me what you've been doing with the Wardens. I better not make it hard for you by asking more questions!"

"And you've been in a battle…" she said.

I laughed again, "Yes, but I can't tell you anything about it!"

She returned my mirth, "I guess all we can do is be together for a bit, and be happy about it!"

She was right, so that is exactly what we did.

∞ ∞ ∞

After a day of fellowship with my sis, her Warden companion, Shelratha, appeared and whisked her away. It was time—it was always about time, with the Wardens, it seemed—for all things appointed to get moving. At the same time, Marmor came and 'fetched' me again, and escorted me through the sparkling tunnels that served as the Wardens' thoroughfares.

It was a longer trip than I had remembered taking through the tunnels before, but I knew better than to ask about it. I guess I didn't know well enough, because once we arrived, I had nothing but questions.

"So, what you are telling me is I need to take the Lance and mix it up with the other spearpoints that I will see when I step back into my world, and that is fine, because…" I let my question remain unspoken.

"Because," Marmor replied, as patiently as always, "You will first wash the Lance completely in the water basin, and scrub it, and wash it again. There will be no more blood on it, and at that *point*, anything that was special about it, will be gone."

"And you couldn't have just done this yourself, because…" I continued.

"The things for the Wardens are for the Wardens. The things for Men are for Mankind. And the things for the Angels are for the Angels. We, and they, are not permitted to interact with the things of your world, unless we have received a special dispensation. No such dispensation was received, so the task falls to you," he explained.

"The Lance will be nothing special once I've cleaned it?" I pressed.

"Of course not. Mankind often has sentimental attachments towards objects, and this is not their fault, as their affinity to the natural order follows from the fact that they were made from the dust of the natural order. Yet, there is no 'magic' to their objects or even to relics. The blood of Christ, however, has power, as it was written, 'The life of a creature is in its blood.' And he was no ordinary creature. So, clean the Lance, and be done with it, and if its enemies ever find it, it can do no harm," he said.

"O.K., if you say so," I said, stepping through the sky-crack that bridged our two worlds.

As before, I was deposited into a room with stone walls lit by torches that bore all the signs of being an armory of some sort. My perception was adjusted, however, when I saw that certain sections were roped off. It was a museum more than an armory. Marmor stood guard in the fissure as I took the Lance over to a nearby sink—there was running water, here.

I was about to put the Lance under the stream when I was struck with a thought: "The enemies of the Lance might use the blood on it for harm, but could I not use it for good? What if… what if I drink some of the bloody water myself?" I put a stopper in the drain as I pondered it.

Then I smelled freshly baked bread and rebuked myself, and it was as if a shadow fled me. I unplugged the sink, and rinsed and scoured the Lance until it was spotless. To be completely honest, it was doubtful that any blood could have been salvaged from the Lance except by extremely tedious retrieval methods using modern science. What had really happened, I suspected, whether this was intended, or not, was that I had been tested. And I only barely passed.

But I *did* pass.

As I stepped back through the gate, I took another look around the room. In my opinion, it had the trappings of being located in Central or South America, sporting weapons and gear of colonial-era Spanish warriors. I felt bad for anyone wandering around the Mediterranean looking for the Lance. "Now let them try to find it!" I chuckled. Then I was gone.

CHAPTER 12

When at last Marmor took me back to the estate, I felt completely rested and refreshed. Breathing the air of the Warden-Realm and being on the receiving end of their healing arts certainly had much to do with that. It was more than that, though. I had lived through an extremely stressful experience and had witnessed horrible things while my own life was in constant danger, and yet I had not merely survived, I succeeded in my mission. I had striven with men, and I thought perhaps with more than that, and had prevailed. I, the formerly scrawny, had acquitted myself in combat with grown men.

The rise in my self-confidence couldn't have come at a better time, as Mr. Chaffee interrupted my studies not long after they had re-started, bringing orders for a new mission. First, he de-briefed me. I cannot lie. I relished telling of my adventures. The only thing I left out was my moment of temptation and how I nearly faltered. He also shared with me what happened to him and Myrtle after we got separated.

Mr. Chaffee narrated: "Once we realized that we were not going to be able to find you, and once we found a place of refuge, we pondered what to do. In the end, we chose to follow a plan similar to yours. However, when we arrived at the Cathedral of Saint Peter, we found it very busy, just as you did. Myrtle wanted to go in, anyway, but I knew that a woman would stand out far too much in that setting. Not long after this, we caught sight of you sneaking into the cathedral. We decided to keep watch for you as well as we could. While doing this, we noticed someone who didn't seem to belong. Like us, his interests appeared to be different than the Crusaders.

"When you finally emerged, we noticed quickly that he noticed *you*. He attempted to follow you, but that night we caught up to him. There was a big fight. We made a lot of noise, but none of us were harmed much, and after a fair bit of that, he ran off into the dark. So, now we had lost you, and we had lost your stalker. Myrtle was quite sure that the stalker was in cahoots with Draco, so we treaded very carefully. However, we never did see Draco.

"That left us to guess what your plan might be. At first, we thought maybe you were going to try to sneak into the Crusaders' quarters while they were sleeping, and steal away the Lance. We even considered doing this, ourselves. It was much too chaotic for that, so we abandoned that thought. We re-traced what we remembered of the event... which was a surreal experience, since Myrtle was actually alive at the time, and had heard details of it, firsthand... and concluded as you did that there was at least one more place and time we could definitively place the Lance.

"Like you, we made for the Bridge Gate. Now, as

we watched the Crusaders muster for battle, we saw Draco's man again. We never saw you, but we felt that he had. Anyway, we weren't going to leave it to chance. After a long and arduous process, we were in reach of the man again. We couldn't very well tussle with him in broad daylight surrounded by knights and soldiers, so instead we constantly harassed him as he tried to thread his own way through the masses. We poked and pulled at him. Myrtle yanked his hair. I got close enough a couple of times to thump him hard. I don't know if he had in fact seen you, but I'd like to think that we helped delay him in finding you, which it seems from your account he finally did."

"Did you see me fighting with Raymond and the man?" I asked.

"I did not," Mr. Chaffee said. "The battle was in full swing at that time. The only thing we could think to do, then, was hope you were having better luck than we were, and try to get ahead of history again. While we didn't have anything near as definitive as the Lance heading out to war out of the Bridge Gate, we knew it was still probable it would show up again as the warriors advanced. We knew they would succeed, even if they didn't. So, we moved north along the city walls to try to be ready to seize an opportunity. But we never spied the Lance."

"What about the White Cavalry? Did you see them?" I asked. O.K, so that was another thing I hadn't shared… that I was sure I had seen the eyes of my deliverer once before.

"Sort of," Mr. Chaffee replied. "We were to the north at that time, as I said. When the tide of battle changed, I could see that white-clad horses were in the mix, but until you shared your story, I would never have suspected they hadn't been part of the Crusader army all along."

"What do you make of the Crusaders around me calling out the names of the saints?" I probed. "Do you think it was really them? They were all supposed to have died hundreds of years earlier."

Mr. Chaffee shrugged, "You and I have seen too much to simply dismiss the possibility. History is stuffed with such accounts. Perhaps Myrtle can give you the definitive answer, but for my part, all I can say is that we were too far away to be able to help you evaluate that matter."

"Alright, so what happened after that?" I asked.

"Well, one of the Wardens came and fetched us, and brought us back. He told us that you had succeeded but had been injured and would need healing. It was just a matter of waiting for you to arrive."

"What of this new mission, then?"

"This is a very simple task. It will be far less intense than your last one, that's for sure!" he replied.

I didn't know if that was a good thing or a bad thing. He continued.

"That man who attacked you while you slept a year ago? We believe we have tracked him to Missouri. In particular, the Branson area. As you are the only one to have seen him, except, perhaps, for Sydney, we are sending you to pick up the scent. Only you will be able to identify him for us. Once you verify that the man we are tracking is the very same as the one that attacked you, you will send word to us, and we will handle it from there."

"Sounds a bit boring," I said.

Mr. Chaffee smiled, "Myrtle and I both hope very much that it is. But you will get to sleep in hotel rooms and eat at restaurants the whole time, so I don't think you will complain too much. And you won't be going alone, either. Patterson will accompany you. I expect that you will have a fine time."

"Yes," I agreed, "this is sounding fabulous. When do we leave?"

"Very soon," Mr. Chaffee replied. "Pat will be here in a day or two with all the provisions you'll need, including the wheels to get you to your destination."

"Excellent," I said.

"There is one more thing, Casey," Mr. Chaffee said, letting the statement linger.

"And it is?" I queried.

"When all this started… I mean, after you became associated with Myrtle and then agreed to join her in her work... there was the thought that you would chiefly be one to assist in the reading and research needed to help others take more direct actions. However, thanks to your father's wise interventions, and perhaps in accordance with higher plans, you are poised to someday be part of those 'direct actions.' You get to decide: will you be a scholar, or will you be a warrior? Think on it, as your future trajectory depends on your answer," Mr. Chaffee explained.

"Isn't 'both' a possibility?" I asked.

"Not exactly," Mr. Chaffee said. "It is true that in Myrtle's organization even the warriors are well-educated. They must be, because of the sort of work they do. However, the education they receive is much more narrow, and focused on specific circumstances. The kind of scholarship we thought you would be engaged in is the sort where you might learn a dozen or more languages and spend much of your time doing archeological digs or browsing through the archives of libraries, and exploring the backroom shelves of museums. That kind of scholarship is needed too, desperately. Important battles are won and lost in books and magazine articles. But the time and training for it is no less than the time and training for combat, for it, too, is a combat of sorts, even when those engaged in it do not understand that it is so. So, you must decide."

"O.K. then, I'll think about it," I replied.

"I know you will," Mr. Chaffee smiled. "We all

eagerly wait your decision."

After that, Mr. Chaffee left, leaving me to retreat to the estate's giant library, and curl up with thirty or so books.

CHAPTER 13.

"Caaaaaaaaaaaaaaaaaaaaaaaaaaaaaasey!" Patterson hollered as he caught sight of me. I was as happy to see him as he was of me.

Shaking his hand, I replied, "About time you came by, Pat! It was getting boring around here!"

For all Pat knew, I had spent the last few months reading in the estate's library. As part of Myrtle's Army, he naturally knew quite a bit more about the world than most, up to and including the history of the Two Trees. However, none of them knew about the Wardens, and as it was virtually impossible to explain how I managed a trip to 1098 Antioch and back without mentioning them, that story, and stories like it, could never be shared with him.

"We're going to have a good time, brother," he said. "A little bit of detective work, maybe a little spying, and then we call in the big guns, then done!"

"I hope you agree with me," I said, "that we may as well do the job right. You know, nice and slow, see some sights, that sort of thing."

"You know it, man. They spotted me a ton of cash for this little operation. We're not going to go hungry, that's for sure."

"Excellent," I said. "When do we leave?"

"Tomorrow, man. Bright and early. Ya know, like, 11 a.m.," he laughed. "The Internet says it's 13 hours away. The only question is whether or not we go through Atlanta, or Nashville. Chaffee says traffic in Atlanta is a nightmare, so I say Nashville, unless you have strong feelings about it."

"I have no strong feelings about anything," I told him.

"That settles it, then," he replied, clapping me on the back. "Tomorrow night, we sleep in Nashville. Day after that, we party in Branson until we get good and bored, and catch our man!"

∞ ∞ ∞

I had been on a fair number of road trips in my young life, but this was by far one of the most enjoyable. No parents to tell me what to do. Someone about my age as a traveling companion. And we could stop any time we wanted to get snacks or do whatever we wanted! No need to coordinate the wishes of six other people in the vehicle, either. The wishes of two male teenagers are so similar they may as well be considered as just one man when taking a trip.

In Nashville, Pat let me choose the fast food place we were going to eat at. Once we sat down to eat with our food, he produced a little cup of ice cream and declared, "Happy birthday, old man!"

I looked at him, confused.

"Ha!" he laughed. "Chaffee was right. You plum forgot you had a birthday a month ago. You're sixteen now, man!"

"When you say it out loud, it doesn't seem so

old," I smiled, shoveling the ice cream into my mouth like a boss.

"You know me, I've always been one to exaggerate," Pat chortled.

"Yea, you have," I agreed. He faked like he was going to punch me and I faked like I was going to duck, then we both went back to eating.

We stuffed ourselves so much on junk food that when we got back to the hotel, both of us crashed fast. The next thing I knew, it was morning, and we were back on the road again.

We arrived in Branson in the middle of the evening and to my surprise, my reaction didn't rise to the level of anticipation I had when I started the trip. One day in the car was exciting, but two days were tedious. And when we arrived? People, *everywhere*. The streets were crowded, the restaurants were packed, and the lines were long. It didn't take long for me to become more than a bit ornery. Pat seemed charged up by everything and didn't seem to be put off one bit by the press of people. In *my* mind, I kept comparing the flush of tourists, with their gawdy clothes and booming voices with the great mass of Crusaders I had been counted with just a month or so earlier. Their solemn assembly and grizzled appearance as they steadily marched into the face of mortal danger made it hard for me to forgive these Americans for reveling in shallow entertainment and indulging in instant gratification.

Now, even as I thought it, I knew I wasn't being fair to the people crushing in around me. I even checked my condemnation for them with the thought that in a way, it was a nice testimony to the fierce protection given to them by the country's armed forces every second of every day, that so many of them could partake in such vacuous activities, with nary a concern for their lives. Still, no matter what mental gymnastics I put myself through, I couldn't feel the same electric thrill that Pat seemed to be riding.

"What's wrong, man?" he inquired.

I shrugged. "Just tired, maybe. Or maybe I just didn't realize I wouldn't like being around so many people."

It was true: I didn't like being surrounded by cacophony. I was as surprised as anyone. I figured I was going find the whole thing exhilarating. Instead, my mind kept going back to those thirty books and how I missed them so much. As we waded through the crowds, I had flashes of memory of the sounds of combat and the stench of spilled blood. It appeared that my adventures had left a mark on me that I had not anticipated and had not noticed until now.

"O.K., O.K., man. Let's move out of the center of all this. There has got to be somewhere a little quieter on the edge of this place," he said. I nodded at him, gratefully.

I have no idea what direction we went or where we were in the town, but we stumbled upon an ice cream shop a bit off the beaten path, and there we encamped. The shop had taken measures to make it seem as though it was straight out of the 1800's, which of course was nonsense, but I still found the wood-paneled walls and hardwood flooring somehow soothing. I started with a hot fudge sundae and after a brief break, went right for the large chocolate shake. Pat was inhaling his share of extremely sugared dairy at about the same rate.

"Now, this is more like it," I said, slurping down the last of my shake.

"As fine a way to end a day as any other," Pat said, leaning back in his seat and rubbing his belly.

"Thanks for making the effort," I said. "I'm sorry I was crabby."

"No big deal. Tomorrow we'll start hunting down your attacker. Soon as we get that wrapped up, we can have another night on the town and do it proper. Or—" and here he winked at me, "—you can stay in the hotel while I trip the light fantastic!"

"Deal!" I declared.

CHAPTER 14.

The sole clue that we had to work with was a scrap of paper that was legible enough only to indicate the name of a street, and the zip code. The house number could not be gleaned nor the name. While this was a very helpful clue in narrowing down the search, it was useless for identifying my attacker, since with no other information in hand, I was the only one who could make the identification.

That is why the following morning, Pat and I were sitting in a car parked on a certain Fisher Street in one of the western suburbs of Branson. I don't know if real stakeouts were like this one, but this one was a blast. Donuts. Hot chocolate. Bags of chips and pop stowed in the back for later. And, a top secret mission. It was almost everything my body could crave.

Whenever we saw someone leave their house, Pat would size up whether or not the person could have been my attacker. If it was, he'd give me the binoculars and I'd have a look.

"You got the phone number in case we spot him?" I asked Pat.

Pat patted his shirt pocket. "Have no fear, Casey dear."

I smirked, surreptitiously checking out another person Pat had selected for me to look at. "Nah. Tall enough, but no beard. Short hair."

"Maybe he shaved and cut his hair?" Pat rejoined.

"He didn't strike me as the kind of guy to do that sort of thing," I said, recalling as I did the distinct smell the man had brought with him.

"Alright, let's watch this block another few hours then have lunch. Then we'll try another block until dinner. Then come back tomorrow to a new section, and do the same thing."

"It's a plan," I agreed.

We followed this plan for several days until it occurred to us that the guy we were looking for might not operate during normal business hours. Reluctantly, we altered our schedule so that we worked some of our previous areas in the early morning and late at night. It was in the dead of night on our fifth day of this when suddenly the back door of the car opened, and someone was in the vehicle before we even had a chance to swing our heads.

"Gentlemen," said a familiar voice.

"Jorge!" I cried out.

Pat was furiously cleaning up the coffee he had spilled in his lap, "Why did you go and do that? You could have knocked on the door or something!"

Even in the pitch of night, there was light enough from the car's radio to reveal Jorge's grinning face in the back seat. "This was much more entertaining!" Jorge said.

Pat replied with something foul and I giggled in spite of myself. "What are you doing here, Jorge?" I asked.

Jorge's tone turned serious, "I've got good news and I've got bad news. What do you want first?"

"I need some good news," Pat growled.

"The good news is, I'm your back-up," Jorge replied.

"And the bad?" I asked.

"You're going to need it."

∞ ∞ ∞

Jorge instructed us to call off the stake-out and rest up for a day. After that, we were to meet him at one of Branson's many gimmicky tourist attractions for a proper briefing. Initially, we were put off by having to wait that long, but after our week of weird hours, it was kind of nice to get our body 'clocks' back to normal before doing anything too adventurous.

My new vigor was sucked from me as we waded through the thick crowd of people. It was a food court of sorts, which lifted my spirits somewhat. Pat and I split up briefly to secure snacks per our own distinct likings, then found a table to eat at and wait for Jorge to arrive. We had finished eating and were contemplating eating again when Jorge plopped down in a chair across from us.

He was wearing a dark suit and sunglasses, looking perfectly comfortable. The man was just *cool*.

"Again, no proper greeting," Pat shook his head. "You could let us see you coming, ya know."

"No fun in that," Jorge grinned again.

Further 'pleasantries' were exchanged and then Jorge got down to business.

"So, here is the deal, gentlemen. I can tell you who this man is and where we can find him. You may have been told that once you located him, you were going to call it in. There has been a change of plans. No need to call, because we are here. And the two of you are going to help apprehending him."

"We?" Pat asked.

"You'll meet the rest at the right time," Jorge said.

"But why? Why are we involved? I don't know that I care, I am just curious," Pat pressed.

"Myrtle has her reasons, as you know. That's the way she rolls," Jorge said.

"I don't think we have been trained for that sort of work," I countered.

Jorge gave me a strange look before saying, "Haven't you?"

"Barging into a house and basically kidnapping a guy? Pretty sure not," I said.

He shrugged his shoulders. "Ah, well, we're not getting him from his house. Sure enough, he has a residence on that street you guys were parked on, but that's not where he spends most of his time. It isn't a house we are snatching him from. It's a cave!"

Pat's face brightened up, "A cave? That could be fun."

"Yes, it could be," Jorge agreed. "But that is not

the really fun part!"

"And that is?" I asked.

Jorge lowered his sunglasses so his eyes could convey the deadly seriousness of his reply.

"Inside that cave… *there be dragons!*"

I about fell off my chair upon Jorge's declaration. Meanwhile, Pat leaned back in his chair, skeptical. It was not the mention of dragons that floored, me, though. *It was those eyes.* I knew I had seen them before! It was Saint George sitting across from me!

CHAPTER 15

George's own expression told me that he knew very well who I was, as well. Pat, naturally was oblivious to this new development swirling about him. Had he known who Jorge really was, he would have dropped all doubt that there really was a dragon in some cave in the area, but since he didn't, he announced that he was going to need another round of snacks if he was going to sit and listen to 'tall tales.' He left the table to fetch more food.

With Pat away, I rushed to the point, "Saint George? *Thee* Saint George?"

He returned my gaze, "The one and the same. I never forget a face, Casey. I've seen millions of them in my time, and I remember them all. When I saw you a few years ago, I knew that you were the one I saved on the plains of Antioch."

"A few years ago? It was only a few months ago that you were training us."

"I first saw you at Myrtle's funeral. The moment I saw you, I realized I was looking at the younger version of that young man grappling for the Lance a thousand years ago. Younger, and much less physically prepared, I'll add," Jorge explained. Before I could comment on that remarkable statement, he continued, "I wasn't the only one to see you there. Your attacker did as well. That is when his hunt began."

"You know *my* attacker?" I asked incredulously.

"I do, indeed. In fact, it is because I tipped him off about where you lived that he knew how to find you to attack you," Jorge said.

Shocking revelation rained down on me after shocking revelation. Was Jorge a 'good guy' or a 'bad guy?' But as I was sitting in stunned silence, he continued his narrative.

"I knew that there was no way you would be capable of succeeding in your Antioch mission without considerable training, but I knew from our encounter in Antioch that you had received that training. So, I watched you from afar, waiting to see when your training would begin, guessing correctly that I would be asked to help you in that training. Month upon month went by with no sign that such things were in the works, so I accelerated things a bit. I tipped off your hunter about your location, knowing that afterwards, your wise father would not allow you to continue in Myrtle's care without equipping you for all of the risks that went with it."

"I could have been killed!" I snapped at him.

"Nonsense," he replied, coolly. "As I said, I knew we would meet in Antioch, so I knew you would not be seriously harmed."

But I was not finished being angry, "And what about my sister, Sydney?"

George's expression changed drastically, "Your sister?"

The instant he said it, I knew that he knew nothing of it, which meant he might not know of the Wardens. I knew I needed to regain my composure and speak carefully. "She's fine," I snarled. "But she almost wasn't."

"I'm sorry, Casey," he said. "I did not know that detail. Believe me when I say that had I known about that, I would have taken additional precautions."

I could tell from his face that he was genuinely sorry. I couldn't resist the urge to forgive him on the spot, and gave into it forthwith, "I forgive you, George. I do."

He looked completely relieved and refreshed but then his serious tone of voice returned, "Now, I am about to tell you something, Casey, which you must not tell Pat and you definitely cannot tell Myrtle or anyone in her organization about."

"Go on quickly, then, before Pat gets back," I prompted him.

"It is simply this: just as Myrtle has an organization, so do I. I am one of her kinsmen who ate some of the fruit of the Tree of Life when she and Draco first distributed it. I, and several others you might recognize, have been living this long time without her being aware of it. Her organization destroys such trees, and sometimes we help her. But you will quickly surmise that we have our own tree, which she does not know about. Just as she keeps her tree closely guarded from Draco, we keep ours guarded from him… and her. Thus, we have a mutual cause and enemy, but we must proceed judiciously. Plus, we have other priorities that she does not know about."

"Why are you telling me this at all?" I asked him.

"You are a man of many secrets already," he said. "As soon as I saw you, I knew that we would one day meet, and inevitably, you would recognize me. You are a bright lad. You would have easily put the pieces together and before I knew it, the relationship I maintain with Myrtle and her organization would be broken into pieces. Just as you protect those you love by keeping her secrets, you protect others by keeping my secrets. I hope you will trust me," he concluded.

"I'm ninety-five percent there," I told him. "But how then can you talk to Pat about dragons?"

"Ah, yes. Well, it's like this," he said. "Everything else about this operation is something that Myrtle's secret-keepers already know about, or can be explained within the framework of knowledge they already possess. Literally the only part she does not know about is that some of the people who ate of the fruit still remain. To be perfectly honest, I think she strongly suspects it, but I am reasonably confident she doesn't know it with certainty. Just as she fakes her death every now and then in order to perpetuate her lineage, we do something similar. We are very careful to stay on the fringes of her organization, though. If she interacted too closely with us, she'd smell us out right away. At the present moment, we pass ourselves off as experts in medieval weaponry and fighting with blades. Myrtle is only one of our clients. We often consult with Hollywood movie makers! You probably know of some of our work."

George leaned back in his seat, brimming with self-satisfaction, but seeing that I had no idea what he was talking about, he continued, "Look, Pat is coming back now. I humbly and earnestly ask that you will not share with him anything about my heritage or the true purpose of my organization, and continue calling me by the name 'Jorge.' Can I count on that?"

I nodded. I didn't like to deceive anyone, but I knew well what Myrtle would do if she learned George's secret. She'd use that information to begin an earnest search for the Tree that was sustaining George and his companions and stop at nothing in that search, until at last, finding it, she would destroy it. "So, about these dragons?" I asked.

"Let's wait for Pat," he said.

Pat arrived, sat down, and began eating fries, "Dragons, then? That sounds made up."

"Does it?" George replied. "You believe that there was once a Tree of Life that has invigorated Myrtle for thousands of years. You believe that her husband has been at war with her for the same stretch of time.

You believe that Draco seeks out these trees for his own purposes, and you believe that he is constantly on the quest for the very blood of Jesus, whether in the grail or elsewhere. And if you believe all that, you believe that Jesus is who he says he is, which means there are a great many other things you should be ready to believe."

"But *dragons?*" Pat said, munching away.

"Surely you know that just as the entire earth is littered with ancient stories bearing testimony of a great deluge, the entire earth has stories of large 'lizard' type creatures. These put the lie to the truly fantastic and unbelievable notion that all these things came about over the eons, and further insists that what we now call 'dinosaurs' never co-existed with Mankind. They cannot accept these many accounts, despite them being old, varied, and independent from each other, for the simple reason that to do so would be to bring their entire worldview down around their ankles. They claim to be driven by evidence, but they ignore whole swathes of evidence for the very simple reason that they cannot abide the implications. But you, my dear friend, should know better," George chided him.

Pat shrugged, "O.K., dragons then." He took a large bite of his hamburger and waited for George to continue. Pat had not chosen the path of scholarship in Myrtle's organization, but the probable existence of dragons, at least in the not-too-distant past, was something that had come up in his training, so why belabor the point?

Bemused, George continued, "Have you heard of the Fisher King?" Neither of us had, so he explained. "The short story is this: Joseph of Arimathea took the Holy Grail to Britain, where it was entrusted to a certain Caradog, son of Bran, the king of a place called Siluria. The grail passed from father to son for generations, until it fell into the possession of one of his descendants. This man would become the one known as the Fisher King. He was not the last in the line of British kings, but he was the last trustee of the Grail. We believe that he has drunk from the Grail, and now lives forever, much like Myrtle. Her life must be refreshed on a regular basis, but the Fisher King's life springs from a better source, the blood of Christ himself. He hides the Grail now, here, in this area."

"Um, in a tourist trap in Missouri?" Pat laughed.

George looked at Pat, hard. "And what is the name of that 'trap'?"

"Branson," Pat chuckled again.

I almost leapt out of my seat. "Holy cats," I blurted out. "Bran's *Son*."

"Now you've got it," George said.

CHAPTER 16.

Questions flooded my mind, but George insisted that he explain the rest while on the way. We dropped our vehicle off at our hotel. George met us there in his SUV and drove us out to a cabin in the woods that he informed us would be our staging grounds. Once there, he filled us in on some other important details.

"Now, the Fisher King is an ornery fella," George said. "He doesn't like it when others seek the Grail, and if he ever thinks someone might be getting close, he'll take steps to intervene. He is not above murder. He operates alone as near as we can tell, so that limits the damage that he can do. It also limits his ability to protect himself and the Grail. We have good reason to believe that Draco or his agents, or both, are on his scent. They may be here, even as we speak."

"If I have this straight," I said, "you're going to put just the three of us up against a dragon, the Fisher King, and Draco and his men?"

"Don't worry, we have help. The Fisher King's cave is being watched and we have scouts scattered around the area watching for Draco," George replied.

"Shouldn't we be calling in reinforcements?" Pat said, fishing out his paper with the phone number on it.

"You could make that call, but you'll just be told that *we* are your reinforcements," George said. "When I say we have help, I mean it. Just because you can't see them, doesn't mean there aren't a lot of capable men ready to spring into action at just the right moment."

"O.K., so how about this dragon, then?" Pat said. "If dragons are around, why haven't we heard more about them? And what does a dragon have to do with this, anyway?"

"Dragons are very rare, but there is an intelligence about them similar to that of wolves. They stay as far away from people as they can. They move only at night, when they move at all. The so-called 'Mothman' was probably a dragon. Many UFO sightings are dragons in flight. We don't know how the Fisher King came in possession of one, but he did. One does not just keep such a creature for fun, so we think this is a firm reason to believe that the Grail is here, and the Fisher King is using the dragon to protect it," George explained.

"In *Branson?*" Pat shook his head incredulously.

George was getting a little irritated at Pat's skepticism. "Almost anything is possible if even half of the old stories be true," George said. "The fact is, we know that this area was founded by a man by the name of Branson, but where he came from ultimately is a bit of a mystery. Personally, I believe it was the Fisher King himself. It is a fine way to hide in plain sight, if you ask me. With all the bells and whistles around the place, it is easy to explain away strange happenings. Be that as it may, he is here, and he likely has the Grail, and he is using a dragon to keep it safe."

"Just how does one kill a dragon, anyway?" I asked.

George looked at me thoughtfully. "That is a good question. It obviously depends on the nature of the beast. Did you know that the very name 'Draco' is derived from the word, 'dragon?' And indeed, in a very real sense, that man is a 'dragon.' The Scriptures, as you know, refer to a dragon that enslaved the whole earth. There was symbolism wrapped in that one, but that is not to say there isn't a deep truth to it. The dragon that we may have to fight is just another beast of creation, an animal, albeit one with a certain cleverness and, how shall we say it?—a foul disposition."

"You were going to tell us how we kill it?" Pat laughed.

"Right!" George chuckled. "I was getting to that. My point was that just as there are many kinds of dogs, there are many kinds of dragons. How we might catch a wolf or coyote is different than how we'd catch a poodle. Until we see it, we won't know what will be required. We will use swords and spears if we have to, but hopefully your standard high-powered elephant rifle will do the trick."

Pat was enjoying the whole thing as if it was a giant running joke. "Well, at least we know then that they don't actually breathe fire!"

"You should just be happy it comes out the front, and not the back, like the bombardier beetle's," George smirked.

"Uh, wait a sec. You're saying…" Pat stammered.

"I'm saying we won't know until we see it," George said. "Don't worry, they can be killed. We've done it." Then he caught himself, and said, "History says it's been done."

"When do we start?" I asked.

"Tomorrow morning," George said. "Provided our spies indicate the Fisher King is still in his cave and that there is no sign that Draco or his men have zeroed in on us, spelunking we shall go."

∞ ∞ ∞

The next morning, George took us on a short trip through the woods where there was another cabin, but this one had a large shed near it. He took us right to the shed upon arrival. Stepping through the door revealed a great sight: about thirty men, girding for battle.

There was a diverse array of weaponry about and the men were not uniformly dressed. A small handful were as you might have expected, wearing SWAT-style gear with bullet-proof vests and submachine guns. Most of them, however, were equipped to fight something other than Man. They actually looked more like firemen, although their clothing was more rigid, as if it doubled as armor. They all wore similar helmets, even the 'tactical' guys. The helmets resembled that of medieval knights. I thought they were all very cool and burned with excitement when it became apparent that I would be wearing similar gear.

Pat opted for the SWAT-style gear, but I put on the fireproof outfit. George handed me a sword in its sheath When I had a free moment, I stole glances at the men around me. I became quite convinced that I had seen some of them, before, as well. No doubt at least a couple of them were some of the saints I saw ride into the Seljuk lines in Antioch. For all I knew, they all were.

Eventually, everyone was geared up, and Pat sauntered over to me, pleased as punch to be included in such an adventure. "There is just one thing, Casey," he said.

"What's that?" I replied.

"Why us? They didn't need us around for this," Pat said.

But George was listening nearby, and interjected. Putting one hand on each of our shoulders he said to us, "I trained the both of you personally, did I not? Few people have the skillset required to do this work—" and here he looked directly at me, "—and few have the variety of experiences that uniquely equip them for it."

"Good enough for me," Pat beamed.

"Good!" said George. "The moment has arrived!"

George led Pat away to group up with the guys resembling SWAT officers. Then he came back and got me.

The answer to Pat's question that George had provided didn't sit right with me, so I pressed George on it now that we were alone. "Seriously, you didn't need us for this. Myrtle and Mr. Chaffee made it sound as though Pat and I were going to do nothing except identify my attacker. Now we are going into danger?"

"How is it that you came to Branson in the first place?" Before I could answer, he offered his own explanation, "Is it not because we made sure that Myrtle's organization knew where to look for that scrap of paper that led you here? And why you? Because *I* wanted you here. Myrtle knows very well what is going on here, which is why she sent me. She trusts me. You should too."

He had a point, so I decided to drop it. It didn't seem to add up, but I knew it wasn't my job to do the arithmetic. Seeing that I was appeased, he brought me to one of the others dressed in the fire-armor, and introduced us.

"Casey, this is Theo. You've met!" George winked. Of course. Saint Theodore, last seen in Antioch.

We shook hands, and I said, "Judging from the

gear, I guess it's a foregone conclusion that this is a fire-breathing dragon we're after."

"Heaven alone yet knows," Theo replied, "but we always take every precaution!"

Introductions over, I followed them out the door. About half took a long lance in hand from a pile that I hadn't noticed before. I was given one, too. It was about twenty feet long, so once we each had our lances in hand, we had to thread our way along the forest path very carefully. Ahead of us, the ones who did not take a lance but had swords only, blazed a path. Pat and the SWAT guys fanned out behind us and I quickly lost sight of them.

Finally, I saw ahead of us a towering stone edifice. When we got closer still, I was able to make out where a gap in the rock wall was apparent, despite someone's attempt to conceal it with branches.

Theo whispered to me, "That's a sizable entrance we're looking at there. A very large dragon could fit inside that cave. Be ready."

Saint George the Dragon-Slayer crept up to the cave entrance, which actually began about five feet off the ground. He stood on his tiptoes and looked into the cave as far as he could see. He gestured behind him, and a squad of swordsmen climbed up and into the cave, disappearing quickly into the black. By this time, the SWAT guys had caught up to us, although I did not see Pat anywhere. Theo and I stood where we were, with about a dozen other warriors encircling the cave entrance. Taking my cue from them, I had my lance angled up towards the entrance, presumably just in case the dragon came flying out unexpectedly.

After what seemed like eternity, one of the swordsmen peeked his head out of the cave entrance and motioned to George, who went to him. The two conferred for a bit, and then George came to the rest of us.

"About one hundred feet in the entrance widens considerably and Gaius says that there is room enough for us to deploy our lances and fight a dragon if need be. I'll go first with a few men, and Theo, you follow with the rest, and Casey," he said.

I breathed in deep before I took my turn entering the cave. The fresh scent of the woodlands was soothing. It disappeared steadily as I went deeper and deeper into the cave, replaced by a mossy coolness which was relaxing in a different way. It was hard to imagine that in such an idyllic setting, war could break out at any moment.

CHAPTER 17.

Our flashlights guided us down the cave corridor to the large clearing that was already well-secured by the time I arrived. The soldiers had set up powerful lights which illuminated the space completely. It was indeed large enough to do battle in. It was about half the size of a football field, and high enough that I could have swung the lance I was carrying over my head if I needed to. After I acclimated myself to the cavern, I noticed that on the opposite end were another two large portals into the deep recesses of the earth. The soldiers were setting up at each one of them as if out of each a mortal threat could be revealed at any moment.

Not long after I came on scene, I was joined by all except the squad securing the cave entrance, and a meeting was held. I stood aside as George, Theo, and some of the other captains plotted their next steps. I thought it likely that two of these were the saints Mercurius and Demetrius, but I had not yet been introduced to them by name.

"Well?" George was asking. "Do we know which tunnel holds our prize?"

Someone I didn't know replied, "It smells fairly foul whichever way you go."

"What are our thoughts about sending parties into each one to find out properly versus staying put at the chokepoint and waiting for them?" George asked.

"I wouldn't want to split up our forces," another man said. "If we were going to explore the tunnels, I'd like to do it one at a time."

"Will take longer," a third said.

"But our radios don't work down here. The party in the false tunnel won't know that a battle has erupted behind it. When they finally return, who knows what they will return to," Theo chimed in.

The third man added, "Also, it could be that the dragon is down one tunnel but the Fisher King is down the other. Two battles could break out, and the rest of us wouldn't even know it."

"We won't belabor it, then," George said. "Mark, assemble a team and pick one of the entrances to venture into. We will finalize our defenses here. I assume our game plan here is the ol' rope-a-dope?"

"Yep. Best way to do it with a dragon," Mark said.

"Good luck, then," George said. The meeting dispersed with each of the men leaving to issue orders and guidance to the men they were in charge of. I watched as the one called Mark gathered his team, organized his supplies and weapons, and disappeared into one of the holes. After he was gone and George had finished some of his own errands, he circled back to me.

"Rope-a-dope?" I asked.

"A boxing term for a historically common military technique. They'll let the dragon push them back through the tunnel until at last they are back in this clearing, where our extra manpower and room for maneuverability will let us battle it properly. These tunnels here are fairly spacious, but who knows how constricted it will get. You want room to move when fighting most dragons," George explained.

"Why are they as worried about fighting the Fisher King as they are fighting a dragon?" I followed up.

"The Fisher King is indeed just one man, and a mere mortal, but he has been around for a very, very, long time. He is a very experienced fighter and knows very well what he must do to survive if he is vastly out-numbered. He fights as fiercely as any dragon and is as slippery as one, too. Our best hope with him is to try to coax him into just giving us the Grail. Probably won't work. He's the most stubborn man alive. Yet, it is worth a try," George smiled.

"I get the impression you have crossed paths with him many times," I said.

George nodded. "Indeed. Each of us is more than a thousand years old and have similar interests which brought us to the same place and time on several occasions. But he may not recognize me. Like Myrtle, I try to conceal myself. I change my appearance, my profession, and move around a fair bit. The Fisher King is more mercurial, however. He is too stubborn to change. Instead, he hides in plain sight in areas where someone like himself doesn't stand out too much and his comings and goings do not arouse suspicion. Ports and wharves and that sort of thing have been his preference."

"I've been meaning to ask you about your long age," I said, treading carefully, lest I broach a sensitive topic. George didn't seem concerned about the line of questioning, so I continued, "According to the legends, you were martyred a long time ago. What gives?"

George pulled his collar back. I remembered, now, seeing the scars around his neck. "I wasn't martyred just once, Casey lad. Many times! Most unpleasant, but there it is. They never took the effort to 'unconstitute' me so, well, with the help of my other often-martyred friends, I was, after a time, restored."

"Beheaded and yet lived?" I asked, somewhat incredulously. I mean, I had a similar conversation with Myrtle at one point, but I hadn't really thought through it.

"Just look at who it is we are pursuing right now. The Fisher King, Bran's son," George said. "Perhaps you do not yet know the tale. I assume you don't. He is the descendent of Bran the Blessed, a giant of a man who also had his head separate from his body. His friends carried his head for seven years, during which time he entertained them enthusiastically. Eventually it fell silent, because none of *his* friends knew the whereabouts of a Tree of Life. Such things are regarded as tall tales and baseless myths to our sterile, secular age, but then, though they hope in their heart of hearts that the deep things that stir them are also true, they prefer rather to think they are smarter and more advanced than their own beating souls, and so snuff out any belief that might lead them to full satisfaction of their needs and wants. But you, of course, know better."

"This might sound like a dumb question," I pressed, "but why would you let yourself be killed so many times?"

George laughed, a little too loudly given their situation. "*Let?* It doesn't work that way! But knowing what I know, it would be foolish indeed to deny my Lord and Maker. Still… most unpleasant."

Just then, we heard commotion echoing to us from the main cave entrance, with the sound of gunshots coming right on the heels of the shouting. George flicked his finger in command and one of the soldiers charged back towards the entrance to find out what was happening. From his grim expression, I suspected he already knew.

Before the scout had returned, a commotion was heard from the tunnel that Mark had taken his men down in search of the dragon, the Fisher King, or both. Gunshots could be heard echoing down that corridor, as well.

There were only about twenty of us left in the great cavern. With the calamitous sounds of battle starting from two of the three entrances, with the third unexplored and potentially as dangerous as the other two, the realization came upon all of us, all at once: we were trapped.

CHAPTER 18.

The cacophony of noise from both directions was compounded by the stone walls of the cave, all the more so as the sounds of fighting drew closer and closer to our cavern. George's scout had arrived with word that the entrance guards were retreating from a large force that almost certainly belonged to Draco. From the other direction, an unworldly noise I had never heard before was getting louder and louder, driving Mark and his men back in retreat. It had to be the dragon.

The two fronts collapsed in on us at about the same time. George quickly shunted me and Pat in the direction of the second, unexplored tunnel, and took charge of the men beating back the dragon at the mouth of the first tunnel. The long lances kept the dragon from stepping into their cavern. I could smell acrid smoke mixing with the foulness of the tunnel, and didn't have to be told that this particular dragon was, indeed, a fire-breather. At the tunnel to the main entrance, several men joined the soldiers in keeping back Draco's men. Sharp bangs punctuated that melee, as it seemed that Draco's men were using grenades to force us to retreat from the entrance.

Pat pulled me down behind a boulder, keeping his weapon shouldered and moving his aim back and forth between the two other entrances to the cavern. I was armed only with the lance and a short sword on my hip.

"We should have called that number," Pat huffed, not taking his eyes off the entrances.

Making sure I stay crouched so a wayward bullet didn't ricochet on me, I grunted a noise that meant, "Why is that?"

"I don't think these were our reinforcements at all, and I don't think we were supposed to be part of this operation. After we got ambushed, I got the distinct impression from what some of Jorge's guys were saying that they have their own interests. I don't know. I didn't really have time to ask since I was being shot at," Pat said. He didn't seem to be very happy about being shot at. He was re-thinking his earlier enthusiasm for the operation.

A question surfaced in my mind that I was shocked I hadn't thought about before: George had said that he tipped the Fisher King off about me… what exactly was it about *me* that would interest the Fisher King? I recalled now that just before the Fisher King was going to bury an axe in my head, he had called me a thief. I wracked my brain trying to put the pieces together.

"To be honest, Pat, there have been a few moments when I wondered if these are the 'good' guys or the 'bad' guys. But it was Mr. Chaffee that had Jorge train us, so they can't be all that 'bad,'" I said, hesitantly.

Pat grunted, "Here, take the number and my

phone. See if you can get a signal and make the call."

I obeyed, but as expected, the call didn't go through.

"Write a text," Pat said. "It won't send, but once we get a signal it will hopefully send automatically."

"*If* we get a signal," I said. I typed this message: "Jorge with us. Said from U. Now in trub, fighting draco and a dragon in a cave by Brans. Sitrep BAD. HELP!"

"I think we should bail down this tunnel," Pat said. "Leave these guys to battle it out and try to get back above ground so we can get help."

"I'd feel bad about abandoning them," I said.

"Don't think of it that way," Pat said. "Jorge pushed us over here for a reason. He didn't really think Draco's dudes would be attacking us, even if he did set a guard. He figured we'd be here for the dragon and the Fisher King, and we'd be fine. He doesn't want us to get killed. Situation bad. You can just tell him we did what we thought he wanted us to do."

I wasn't so sure, but Pat was persistent. "O.K.," I said, "But we aren't really prepared. I've got a flashlight and you have the light on your gun, but those won't last. We don't have food or water. We're not going to last long unless we find a way out. If Geo—Jorge and his men are beaten, we'll be next!"

"Fair enough," Pat said, "but we're looking to be next as it is!"

He wasn't wrong. Grenades were now exploding just inside the cavern and bullets were bouncing all around the cavern from the ricochets. I could see men laying on the ground, still, at each entrance. A bullet hit close and I decided it was close enough.

"Let's go!" I shouted. I pulled Pat by the armor on his back and yanked him into the second tunnel. After we went a few steps, I fished out my flashlight and shined it ahead of me.

"Go, go, go!" Pat said, now pushing me down the tunnel.

You couldn't very well run in a cave-tunnel, especially with what little light we had, but we did the best we could. Five minutes later, we had gone far enough that the sound of gunfire and shouting had softened considerably. We stopped for a few moments to take a breath, and then 'ran' for another five minutes.

"Man, it stinks," I said.

"I think that dragon uses both of these tunnels," Pat said, holding his nose.

"I haven't seen any hint of another way out of here," I said.

"Nope. But let's keep going," Pat said. "If Jorge prevails, he will know to come look for us. If he doesn't, there is a slim chance that whoever is left, Draco or the Dragon, will think there is no need to come down this way. We can go quite far. Jorge would not stop looking for us if he's the one still standing."

"Alright, let's go again," I said, accepting his analysis.

Instead of faux-running, we now were jogging. After fifteen or twenty minutes of this, winding our way around turns and curves, some of which were sharp, we could hear no sounds of battle at all. We stopped to take a break again, shining our flash lights around us in search of a way out.

"How far do you think we've gone" I asked him.

"It's gotta be three to five miles. Hard to say with all these twists and turns," he said.

"Think we should stay put?" I asked.

"As much distance as we can. That's what I think. Same reasons as before," he said.

"Alright then," I said. "Break's over. Let's go!" I wasn't eager to keep going. I was eager to get far enough away that Pat would think was safe enough, so we could stop running.

"O.K.," he said, standing.

Then, a bellow I had heard before: "THIEF!"

We trained our lights at the source of the sound and it was, as I expected, the massive hulk of the Fisher King.

The giant was on top of us before Pat could fire a shot. I had long ago abandoned my lance, but I still had my short sword. The Fisher King knocked that away, too. I was in a dark tunnel with the Fisher King yet again. This time, I was bigger and stronger, actually trained, and had something passing as experience in war. I also had Pat fighting with me.

Still, it was just as George had said. The Fisher King had been fighting for more than a thousand years, was larger than both Pat and I, combined... and this time we were in *his* tunnel.

There was punching, kicking, biting, scratching, bending, pushing, throwing, cracking, smacking, and falling. The three of us wrestled in the pitch black in mortal combat. There was no danger of accidentally striking Pat. It was easy to know which body was the Fisher King's.

Then I heard the recognizable sound of a fist hitting a jaw, and I felt Pat slump away. He was out of the fight. It was just me and the Fisher King.

He was strong and powerful, but I was nimble and flexible. He almost always had a grip on me, but I was constantly twisting out of it, and he'd have to get a new grip on me. Scratching, smashing, thrusting, rolling. We were on the ground, now. At one point, I freed up both of my hands and I rained my fists onto his face. I'm sure it hurt him, but I doubt it hurt him as much as it hurt me. Then I felt my fist sink into the cold sand and I knew he had moved his head in the dark. He was laughing even as his lungs heaved, letting me know he was getting out of breath, but at the same time making it as clear as day that I could do nothing to harm him.

My head jerked suddenly, and I yowled. He had

me by my hair and was pulling me along the tunnel. I pounded his arm with my fists and tried to pry his fingers from my hair, but to no avail. Then I hit my shin on a stone in the tunnel and in spite of things, fell to the ground in pain. The new direction of my body must have surprised the Fisher King, too, since he was no longer holding my hair.

There are few things as painful as hitting your shin, but I had no time to deal with it. It was one of the first times that there had been any separation between us, so I rolled away in the dark in a direction that I hoped was opposite the direction of The Fisher King.

"Where are you going, *thief?*" the Fisher King boomed. This time, he had me by an ear. He pulled me up hard, and there was nothing I could do about it. My head followed my ear whether I liked it or not, and my body followed my head for the same reason. Once on my feet, he thumped me good on the side of the head, and that was the end of the fight. Completely disorientated, with pain throbbing from all sides, I couldn't resist him any further. I had some sense that he picked me up and threw me over his shoulder and was carrying me, but soon even that sense was gone. Darkness overtook my mind the way that darkness had swallowed up my body, and I thought no more.

CHAPTER 19.

Long before my eyes opened, I knew I was on a boat. The rocking motion, soothing and undulating, was enough to give it away; however, I could feel droplets on my face and arms, which cinched it. The next thing that presented itself to my senses was the smell of ocean. Finally, sea gulls shouted into my ears, dragging me kicking and screaming out of unconsciousness. Still, I did not open my eyes.

I had been abducted. I was sure of it. If I opened my eyes, my captor would know that I had returned to the world, and I might lose an advantage, if there was in fact one to lose. I used the time to ascertain the status of my body. What were the extents of my wounds? Were there any parts of me that throbbed? Indeed, there were. I discreetly moved my hands and quickly discovered they were bound behind my back. I dared not yet move my feet, but I felt a weight on them, and suspected they were bound, as well.

It was my thirst that got me. My dry mouth and my straining lungs joined forces with my body aches to compel me, against my better judgement, to open my eyes to see what there was to see. I did this as sneakily as I could, lifting my lids just high enough to see what was at my feet. They were indeed bound: with chains. The chains in turn were fastened to the deck of what I imagined was a decent sized fishing boat. I appeared to be propped up in the back corner of the deck. To my immediate right and within my reach was a bench bolted into the deck. Lying on it, likely there to taunt me, was my short sword.

I opened my eyes up completely. It was indeed a fishing boat. I was in fact lodged in the corner, which explained the steady fall of mist on my face. I tugged my hands forward, and now I knew that they weren't merely bound, but chained. Turning my head so my eyes could gather more information, I could see nothing except the horizon on all sides save right ahead of me, where the bridge of the boat was manned by the hulking behemoth I knew to be the Fisher King. He had both hands on the steering wheel and turned his head neither to the left or the right.

After a while, it seemed that he was never going to notice I was awake, and I was going to die of thirst, so I decided I needed to force the matter.

"Hey!" I rasped, "Mr. King? Mr. Fisher? Mr. Fisher King Dude? Can I get some water or something over here?"

The Fisher King casually looked over his shoulder. Without even seeing his face, but just his ears twitching slightly, I could tell he was smirking at my panting. Taking his own sweet time, he lashed the wheel and lumbered down the sea-worn steps, grabbing a pot with him as he went. That action drew my attention to something I hadn't noticed yet. Tucked under the stairs was a bunch of cylinders and containers, including, I realized with a start, a familiar, ancient pot from Jerusalem. It was the very same one from my previous adventure with Myrtle. Jesus' blood had fallen on the ground as he was being taken to the cross, and I had scooped the bloody dirt into the pot until it could hold no more. I was among the few people in all of history that knew that this pot was the actual source for all of the legends about the Holy Grail.

I hoped my captor hadn't noticed my recognition. Questions percolated in my mind: did the Fisher King know what he had in his possession? Did he know that I knew the truth about the Grail? How did *he* obtain it? I forced myself to wear my best poker face until I figured out what the truth of the matter was.

Finally standing in front of me, he tipped the pot he had in his hand to my lips and let me have a deep drink.

"Wah-ish-thap?" I blurted, spitting it out. The foul drink reeked of rotten fish.

The Fisher King threw his head back and laughed and laughed and laughed, his belly shaking so hard that the pot rattled in his hand, sending disgusting drink flying about, with some of it falling on me.

"That there is some good stuff I made myself. Learned it from the Vietnamese!" he bellowed. "Ungrateful. Here, try this."

He tipped another drink in to my mouth. I spat

that out too, and merely glared at him.

"Don't like saki, either?" he said, possibly genuinely disappointed.

"I need water, man. Good old-fashioned H2O," I practically commanded, "preferably before I die."

"You ain't gonna die," he harrumphed. He went into the cabin and returned with an old thermos. "Some water in here," he muttered, putting it to my lips.

Quality-wise, it was the worst water that had ever been in my mouth, but I was so thirsty that in that moment, I considered it the best water I had ever tasted. I should have said "thank you" but I wasn't really happy with the man, as you can imagine. Instead, I glared at him.

"Don't you go looking at me like that, young man," he said sternly, with a smile playing at the corners of his mouth. He went and pulled up a rickety chair and sat down in front of me. I couldn't believe the chair held him.

"Why do you have me chained up?" I demanded to know.

"Ho! Why do I have you chained up?" he shouted. Then he did the whole belly-laugh thing again. "'Why do you have me chained up?' he asks!" He was nearly doubled over in laughter, now. "Look here, young man!"

The Fisher King stood up, pulled his shirt up about as high as it could go, and nudged aside his long and unruly beard. A big black bruise right on his chest, just below the right shoulder, glistened out at me.

I smiled mischievously.

"You're a scrapper, lad. A real scrapper," he grunted. "I can't very well be trusting you to something as flimsy as rope, now, can I?"

"Alright then," I replied, not caring to disagree, "why did you kidnap me?"

"Ungrateful lad! I could have killed you, ya know. I might still! I took ya because I've got questions, and I want answers."

"And *then* you'll kill me," I retorted.

"Might," he smirked.

"You may as well ask them and get it over with, then," I said. "But would it kill *you* to let me eat something? I'm famished."

"I might need that food myself, and if I go and kill you, then it's just a waste, isn't it?" he said. "How about we see how my interrogation goes."

"It's your boat," I snapped.

"That it is," he said, shifting in his chair. He thought for a moment, and then said, "How did Draco find out about me?"

"How should I know?" I shot back. But I also collected my wits a bit, realizing that he would be better than most at piecing together clues. There were things I knew that he might not, but could figure out if I wasn't careful.

"Well, you are Draco's kid, aren'cha?" he replied, his tone of voice suggesting his question was as obvious as the answer.

"I've heard that I resemble him," I said. "I'm not on his side, though. I consider him my enemy."

"Is that a fact? Well, that's curious. Curious, indeed. Very curious," he said, stroking his beard. Then he said, "You was working with him, though. How do you explain *that?*"

"I was not!" I blurted out. "We were coming for you, when Draco's men attacked us from behind."

"And why was ya coming for *me?*" he asked, his eyes narrowing.

"I don't know if I can answer that for everyone else, but I was coming to get some revenge!"

"You're that scrawny lad I tried to bury my axe into, aren'cha?" he said, eyeing me. "I knew it. You looked different, but when I saw yuz, I knew it was you."

I was afraid I had already given too much away, but I resented being taken captive by this big buffoon. I decided to ask a question of my own, if only to provide myself some cover in my future answers.

"When you tried to kill me, you called me a thief," I said. "What was that all about?"

"Well, ya are a thief, aren'cha? Trying to steal the Grail!" He sprang up out of his seat. "Many have tried, but when they get close I break their necks, see? Or bury my blade in them!"

"I don't know what you're talking about," I said, deliberately forcing myself to not let my eyes wander to where the Grail was under the stairs. "I was just lying in bed, minding my own business."

"Nah! I got information. I got information that said you, yes, *you*, boy, was on to me, if not on the way *to* me," he said. "I couldn't fathom it, but no one could have had that information if they didn't know with some detail where I was hiding it."

"Not me," I insisted. "Besides, that was two years ago, now. If I had really known for all that time, wouldn't I had already come for you?"

It didn't seem like the most profound rebuttal, but it did seem to stump him. "Reckon there is some truth to that. Just a little, I wager." He stood up and moved to stow away his chair, then he turned back to me, "You can at least tell me your name, boy, can'cha?"

I shrugged, "My name is Casey."

"Alright," he said. "That's not your full name, of course, but it'll do. Casey it is," he stated. Then he turned to go back up to the cabin.

"Aren't you going to give me any food?" I called after him.

"I still haven't decided if I'm gonna whack ya!" he threw over his shoulder.

From where I sat, I could see everything there was to see. Oceans on all sides, and the Fisher King in his cabin, steering the boat. That was it. Every now and then, the Fisher King changed it up a little and appeared to be consulting charts and making calculations. To really throw some variety in there, he drank some of that disgusting fish drink he had tried to offer me. Otherwise, the next few hours were spent with him at the wheel. As the sun was going down, he lumbered down the steps and once again stood in front of me.

"Good night, Casey. Sleep well. I'll most likely kill you in the morning."

Then he turned on his heels and disappeared into the bowels of the ship, leaving me speechless and stunned, absolutely famished, and getting colder by the minute.

CHAPTER 20.

Even in the summer, it can get quite cool at night on the open sea. I wasn't very happy with the Fisher King when the sun woke me the next morning, but I was sure happy with that sun! After being left out in the cold all night, I decided I wasn't going to let my captor sleep in, so I started making up pirate songs, and singing them loud.

"Yo -ho! And a bottle of rum! The Fisher King and his bottle of scum!" I rasped out as bawdily as I could. I'd repeat a verse about a dozen times, trying to piece something together that was clever in the meantime. "Fisher-me-This, Fisher-me-That! The so-called king is lard and fat!"

I was just getting round to eye patches and peg legs when the Fisher King climbed out of the hold and glared at me. He disappeared somewhere towards the front for a few minutes then came back around to me. To my surprise, he wasn't angry with me. He actually seemed quite pleased with me. He retrieved his bottle of fish sauce and positioned his chair in front of me again. Plunking down, he eyed me seriously.

"You are a real scrapper, Casey. A real scrapper!"

"Let me out of these chains, and I'll prove it to you again," I said.

"Oh ho! I bet you will! But this time you don't have any secret passageways or tunnels to hide in. I got you chained up real good. I could wail on you as you sit, and you couldn't do anything about it!" he chuckled.

"But imagine the violence I'm doing to you in my mind," I snarked.

"Oh, I am. I am," he snickered.

"What are you going to do with me?" I asked.

"Alright, let's talk about that. You said you weren't with Draco. Who were you with?" he asked, eyeing me warily.

I didn't want to give up Myrtle or George or anyone I cared about and I didn't know what the big man knew or didn't know, so I stayed mum. Perhaps guessing the reasons for my silence, he asked a new question. "I know you were looking for the Grail. The funny thing about that is you guys don't even know what it looks like. You'll never find it. Unless I make it plain to ya, you'll never know. It's a waste of your time. For thousands of years, they've been trying. Anyone who got close didn't get any closer, if you take my meaning. But hardly anyone did. You came as close as any of those folks, though, maybe closer. Just how did you do that?"

I felt that it was as risky to not answer as to answer, so I offered, "If so many people keep finding out about it, maybe it needs to be kept in safer hands. What if Draco got a hold of it… and drank from it? Then what would happen to the world? You would have a truly immortal villain causing havoc forever, all because a big buffoon like you couldn't protect it!" I chose my words carefully, as I didn't want him to realize that I knew it wasn't something that anyone could drink.

"Safer hands than mine? For almost two thousand years I've kept it safe. Never lost it. Never will," the Fisher King declared.

"My friends will find me," I said. "When they do, they'll decide for themselves if that's the case."

"Yes, I'm very interested in your friends, I'll get back around to them," he replied. "Let me ask you another question."

He paused to wipe fish sauce out of his mustache.

"Why aren'cha afraid of me?" he asked, leaning towards me menacingly. For a split second I did feel a hint of fear but then gathered myself up, and as far as the chains that bound me would let me, sat up straight, lifted my head high, and jutted my jaw out at him.

"I know all I need to do is call upon the Lord Jesus for help and I will have it," I asserted. "He delivered me from you once, he'll do it again. Either to sail this ship home myself and alone, or to sail to the Undying Lands, further up and further in, surrounded by a great cloud of witnesses. Nothing you can do about it, either!" I didn't know where my confidence or my words came from.

At that moment, the distinct scent of home-baked bread enveloped me, driving out the awful fish smell of the ship entirely.

The Fisher King fell back at my words, but regrouped, and sat still in his chair.

"These are not the words of anyone associated with Draco," he declared. He stood up, and started pacing back and forth, occasionally turning his back to me.

"Truer words you have never spoken," I said defiantly. Even as I said it, one of the strangest things to have ever happened to me occurred. Behind my back, where the side of the ship was, I felt a transformation. For a half second, as I was leaning back against the wall of the ship, it felt as though the wall had de-materialized. Because I had been leaning against it when it vanished, I almost fell out of the boat and into the water, but something caught me and held me up. It seemed to me that a Warden's fissure had opened up where the railing of the ship ought to be.

Then something even stranger happened. I felt a slight tugging at the chains and heard them jingle, ever so slightly. My hands were free! My short sword still remained on the bench near me, almost within reach! I curled my feet back behind me, and I felt the chains drop from my feet, as well. I thought to make my escape via the Warden Realm, but I heard a voice whisper in my ear, "Play the man, Casey," it said. I thought it was Marmor that freed me, but I had never heard him whisper before, so wasn't absolutely certain. Then the fissure was gone, and I knew that my only escape now was that sword and a final battle. But the Fisher King was still speaking.

"These friends you speak of," he said, continuing his pacing. "How do you know that the men in the cavern were not themselves Draco's men, and the men outside the cave fighting to get in were not in fact there trying to save you?"

This was a new thought, and I felt like I had been sucker-punched in the gut. I remembered my own misgivings at the time and then Pat's frantic attempts to explain his unease as bullets and battle raged around us. George had prevented us from making that call—the phone! Did my text go through?—and perhaps it was because George was working with Draco all along. Maybe the Grail wasn't the only prize to be won. Maybe he was after me, too!

It covered the facts just as easily as what I had been led to believe so far. Perhaps Mr. Chaffee, or Myrtle, with all of her manners of gathering information, had concluded that Pat and I were in grave danger. Maybe they determined that 'Jorge' was working with Draco... maybe they already knew this from the start? Might they have sent a rescue party, only to be blocked by none other than one of the persons they were trying to save, none other than Patterson himself, not knowing any better? That could explain the strange comments that Pat said he overheard.

And if… if this be the true account… then I had been deceived! Moreover, it could be the Fisher King was not my enemy. But—he *had* tried…

"But you tried to kill me!" I yelled, leaping up from my place and grabbing the sword in a single motion. Before the Fisher King could react, I had the tip of the blade at his throat. He was so much taller than me that I would have to leap to get purchase on his fleshy neck but both he and I knew I could do it.

"You're a real scrapper, Casey. A real scrapper," he said, beaming at me.

CHAPTER 21

"Give me a reason not to run you through right now!" I yelled.

"Aye, you already have your reason, and you know it," he replied. "You know as well as I do that we both mean to keep the Grail secret and safe. You know as well as I do that the ones you were with were sketchy, on retrospect. You may as well throw your lot in with me, lad."

"What are you proposing?" I barked, leaning the sword even closer, if that were even possible.

"I'm saying... let's you and I join forces. I'll convince you that I mean you no harm, and then maybe the two of us can sort out who friend and foe *really* is," he said.

"Given that you already tried to kill me once and have now kept me without food and water for who knows how long, I don't know how else you can convince me of that than to leap off this ship right now, and swim away," I said.

"Oh, well now," he practically drawled, "a big fellah like me, I'd sink like a rock. How about I do something else, instead... relax, there, lad..."

Gingerly taking a short step backwards, he slowly dropped down to one knee, then the other, and then he leaned over in front of me. Kneeling like this, he then took his tree-trunk arm and he used his catcher's mitt of a hand to pull his long hair aside so

I could plainly see, and reach, his neck. "Now, if this doesn't win your trust, then by all means, aim true—I know the sword is sharp enough and I know you're strong enough. A side benefit is once you're done, I'll still keep you entertained for about seventy years, I reckon."

I let the blade of the sword rest on the back of his neck, testing his bluff, but he remained there motionless.

"Come on, lad, don't take all day. I'm hungry, and I know you are, too. Make up your mind."

"On one condition," I said.

"Name it," he replied.

"Exactly so. How are you named?"

"The long version or the short version," he said, his voice muffled from being so close to the deck of the ship.

I laughed, "The short version will do."

"Not the one on the white stone, then?"

"Come on *lad*, don't take all day," I replied. "I'm hungry, and I know you are too…"

"He's got spirit, this one," he laughed. "It's true enough if you just call me Branson."

"Very well, Branson. Rise, and eat. And I sure hope you got something more than this foul fish sauce for me!" I said, lowering my blade. Then, to seal the trust, I put the sword back on the bench.

Standing up, Branson looked at my sword where I set it, and then to the chains, which lay in a heap where I had previously been imprisoned. "At some point, you're going to have to tell me how you got out of those chains."

I smiled, but said nothing.

"Alright, well, the truth is I don't have anything for you. I've always found this to be quite sufficient. Lucky for you, as you well know, I am a bit of an expert when it comes to fishing. If you just give me a minute..." he said, but hesitating, nodding in the direction of where he wanted to go but not yet moving because he didn't want to cause me alarm.

"You're a free man!" I said.

"Very well. One rod and reel coming up, and fried fish shortly after that!"

∞ ∞ ∞

After Branson landed some fish and fried it up for me, he produced another chair for me and a folding table for me to eat at.

"You're not going to tell me how you got out of those chains, are you?" he asked, as I munched away.

"Are you going to tell me what the Grail is?" I asked, chewing. Not only did Branson land the fish in record time, he managed to catch the tastiest one the sea had to offer, and cooked it to perfection. I could have eaten fish the rest of my life if Branson was the one to catch and prepare it.

"I can't do that," he replied.

"Then I guess we're both men of secrets," I said. "Can you tell me how I got on this boat?"

"I can tell you that much," he said. "Surely you know that someone like myself wouldn't go into a cave with only one way in and out. I left your friend lying there. He's fine, I'm sure. I carried you out the other entrance, tossed you into the back seat of my truck, drove you down to a slip I have in Louisiana, and the rest you know."

"We are in the Gulf of Mexico?"

"Way out in it, yes," he replied.

"So, now what?"

"We're going to need some help sorting this out," he said. "I know a guy."

"He can be trusted?" I asked.

"If you can trust me, you can trust him," he said.

"I suppose we're still working on that. Can you tell me his name?"

"Goes by 'The Bard.' We'll sail on past Florida into his parts, and go from there."

"These 'parts.' Where might they be?" I asked.

"Why, Bermuda, of course. The best place on earth to get lost in, I dare say," Branson said.

"Alright, then, sailor. Set your course for Bermuda!"

"Already did, captain!" Branson laughed. "Here, have some more fish."

I devoured it ravenously, thinking as I did that his fried fish smelled about as good as the best baked bread I'd ever had.

After I had my fill, I tested our trust even further

by creeping up behind Branson while he was at the wheel, and standing next to him. He didn't even flinch. The sun was dead ahead. Though it was riding high in the sky, it still blinded me. The light flashed on the low waves everywhere in front of me. I had to turn away, while Branson continued looking straight ahead, unbothered. He did have a visor blocking some of the sun, but I still couldn't understand how he could stand it.

"There are some sunglasses in that cabinet to your right," he said. I fetched them. The relief was immediate, although the impression that we were sailing on a bed of blindingly brilliant diamonds remained. My eyes adjusted as well as they could and it was good enough for scanning the horizon. Here and there I saw smudges which I took to be other vessels.

Branson broke the long silence, "Tomorrow, we'll be near Florida on the left and Cuba on the right, although you won't be able to see them. But we'll call it a night before passing through them and take the strait. I'm heading for waters that will be less trafficked overnight so I can get some rest. When I sail alone, I have to be careful where I sleep. Gotta stay out of everyone's way. You are too new to be helpful, but we'll train ya up right. Then maybe both of us can get good sleep."

"How long will this take?" I asked.

He shrugged, "So much can happen. Who knows?

These are dangerous waters, to tell the truth. Something bound to happen tonight, even."

"Tonight?" I probed.

"Well, I wouldn't tell ya there are pirates, exactly, but lots of smuggling, for sure. Luckily, they tend to be the sort who want to be left alone, but you never can let your guard down around the criminal-type," he explained.

"Are you worried?" I asked.

The Fisher King smiled broadly. For the first time, I noticed that there was a big golden tooth in Branson's mouth, surrounded by all the ivory ones. "Nah, we've got back up," he said. I waited for him to explain, but he didn't.

The explanation came soon enough. Just as Branson had said, as the sun was setting behind them and dusk had fully set in, Branson spotted a vessel that looked to be coming right at them. "See, there?" he asked. "Up to no good, I reckon."

When the ship was close enough, Branson pulled out his binoculars and gave them a hard look. "Up to no good, indeed," he grumbled.

"What are we going to do?" I asked.

"Only fair to let them get up close so I can warn'em to back off," he said.

"Have we any weapons besides my sword?" I asked.

Branson grinned again.

Finally, the other boat was close enough that even

I could make out the details, despite there only being a little light left. It was only a little bigger than the one that I was on, but I could see the silhouettes of quite a few more people. There were at least a dozen people standing erect on the deck, poised, it seemed to me, ready for action.

Branson called out to them in a big, booming voice, "You ain't gonna get any more warning than this. If you get within thirty feet of my ship, I'm gonna sink ya. So getouttahere!"

There was no doubt that Branson was heard, as his bellow was like a bullhorn. But the boat drew nearer. Within just a moment or so, it would reach the limit Branson had set.

"Try to outrun them?" I asked. I couldn't imagine that Branson had successfully protected the Grail after all these years without weapons or fast vehicles.

"Wait for it," Branson said. I noticed, then, that he had produced a slender rod that I took to be a whistle, and put it to his lips. Once the other ship was within thirty feet, Branson blew the whistle. It was far louder than any whistle I had ever heard. Even the men on the other ship seemed startled, but their boat was now just twenty feet away, and coming closer. In just seconds, they would be boarded.

At that very moment, there was a loud shriek from the sky. All heads looked up except Branson's, who kept his eyes steadily on the other ship. One of the stars seemed to drop from the heavens and rapidly swelled up to the size of a basketball. All of us probably realized at the same time that the light we were seeing was fire. Then, the ball turned into a blazing plume, looking very much what I imagined a flame thrower to look like. The plume raked the other ship, torching it. As the flame veered away, I saw a slender, albeit very large, shadow attached to it, moving rapidly into the sky and circling back.

To my surprise, no one tried to leap off the burning pyre.

"They are already dead," Branson said. "Now watch."

The plume seemed to dissipate as the shadow dropped straight down from the sky. It dove into the burning ship like an arrow passing through a cloud. A great stream of water leapt up from the center of the ship. The shadow re-appeared a hundred yards away and disappeared into the night. The ship, which only seconds before had been an inferno, now sank like a rock. After two minutes, there was no trace of it left.

"What was that?" I said, in awe.

"That my dear Casey, was Cadwallon. My dragon."

I was pretty amped up by what I had just witnessed but Branson didn't want to talk about it. For all his bravado, it seemed he wasn't too pleased to have to end lives, even if they were the sort that would have done far worse to us. With darkness fully upon us and Branson sullen, the rise and fall of the waves made me drowsy enough to sleep. Branson let me sleep in his bed in the cabin. He stayed on watch through the night, alone with his thoughts.

In the morning, he already had fish fried up for me to eat, and I gobbled it up quickly. Then I joined him on the bridge, standing next to him as he stared ahead with both of his hands once again on the wheel.

"A dragon, eh?" I prodded.

Branson beamed. "Cadwallon. Me and him been guarding the Grail together from the beginning… and, well, um, he always keeps an eye on me!"

I knew why Branson had checked himself. If both he and the dragon were here, then it followed that the Grail was very close. This was information that he surely didn't want me to have. For his sake, I played dumb.

"I thought dragons were mythical beasts!" I said.

Branson scoffed at me, "After all ya know, you say such a thing? Surely by now ya know that to call something a 'myth' is not to say it's not true or real. A 'myth' is just a story that some folks think is true. Whether it is or not true is an entirely separate question!"

"On that definition, stories about dragons are stories that you think are true. That would make them mythical, right?"

Branson screwed up his eyes. "Ya got me Casey. But if you're going to do that to me, *you* are a mythical beast too!"

I smiled. I could live with that. "Why don't people see more dragons, though? Where did they all go?" I asked him.

"Most of 'em died in the Great Deluge, of course, along with most other things. But the environment after the Great Deluge was not all that great for creatures like these. I mean, surely you see by now that what they called 'dragons' in the old stories are what some folk call 'dinosaurs' today? Temperamental creatures with unhealthy appetites. I reckon most of them just couldn't hack it after the Flood. But there were still some, to be sure, which is why we gottem in the old stories.

"Back in the day… when I was young, ya see," he said, looking at me from the corner of his eye, "there were far more of these creatures, although fairly rare even then. They steered clear of people if they could, but I tell ya, they got unhealthy appetites, and there ain't nothing more tempting to a dragon than a nice herd of sheep all bunched together. Eat once, sleep for a couple of years after that, with a feast like that."

"And, for the same reason, they were hunted whenever folks knew they were around. A dragon isn't the kind of predator you can get away with leaving alone if you happen to find yourself in his range."

"But what about Cads...wallop?" I asked.

"Cadwallon. Well, you can tame em, sorta, if ya know what you're doin.' My family always had a way with'em. They have a certain intelligence. And, anyway, Cadwallon knows what is going on. He knows his job and why he's doing it. Long story," Branson said.

"Where is he now?" I asked.

"Not far from us at all," Branson smiled mischievously. Evidently that was all he was going to say about the matter, though. "If you find this interesting, wait until we get to Bermuda. Lots of interesting things, there."

"Are you going to tell me like what?" I asked.

"Nope."

"Is there anything you can tell me?" I pressed. The morning sun was in our eyes again. The heat beat on my face, but the mist that was springing up from the hull brought continual relief and renewal. There was a breeze which was soothing as well, but the saltiness and the sound of seagulls stalking us suggested the atmosphere was charged with excitement.

"Only that your adventures have only just begun, dear Casey. Only just begun."

From the author:

I hope you enjoyed *The Fisher King's Apprentice!*

If you want to read more stories from *The Annals of Myrtle and the Blood-King*, you can help spread the word about this book and the series. How? The most obvious way is to talk to people about it!

But I bet you thought of that yourself.

Other ideas:

Books make great gifts! Think about this one for birthdays and Christmas!

Tell your local library that you really, *really*, want the author of *The Fisher King's Apprentice* to come and do a book signing there!

Let your teacher know that you think this would be a fine book to read to the class. Ask him or her, "Have you heard of *The Fisher King's Apprentice* by AR Horvath? I really liked it! You should check it out."

You can also find the author on social media and elsewhere and share the information with others! If you haven't already, pick up the first in *The Annals of Myrtle and the Blood-King*, a book called *The Warden-Watch*, and enjoy and share that one, too!

Then, keep your eyes out for the next in the series!

Yours sincerely,
AR Horvath

www.ingramcontent.com/pod-product-compliance
Lightning Source LLC
Chambersburg PA
CBHW011447170626
46816CB00008B/2552